Praise for Little Boy Lost
by J.P. BARNABY

Enlightened

"*Enlightened* is an incredible story about the power of love and the damage intolerance and prejudice can do."

—Fallen Angel Reviews

"Every now and then a book comes along that you do not want to end…"

—Reviews by Amos Lassen

"A pitch perfect coming of age story. Not to be missed!"

—Reviews by Jessewave

Abandoned

"*Abandoned* is very strongly written, the scene setting, the verbiage, the plot, all of it very well done. I could find nothing wrong within these pages of this strong YA novel."

—Top 2 Bottom Reviews

"This is an utterly realistic, heart-wrenching story about a young boy trying to make his way in the world."

—Queer Magazine Online

NOVELS
By J.P. Barnaby

THE LITTLE BOY LOST SERIES
Enlightened
Abandoned
Vanished
Discovered
Escaped

NOVELLAS
By J.P. Barnaby

Mastering the Ride
Papi

Available from
DREAMSPINNER PRESS

LITTLE BOY LOST SERIES: 5

Escaped
J. P. Barnaby

Published by
Dreamspinner Press
382 NE 191st Street #88329
Miami, FL 33179-3899, USA
http://www.dreamspinnerpress.com/

This is a work of fiction. Names, characters, places, and incidents either are the product of the author's imagination or are used fictitiously, and any resemblance to actual persons, living or dead, business establishments, events, or locales is entirely coincidental.

Escaped
Copyright © 2012 by J.P. Barnaby

Cover Art by Catt Ford

All rights reserved. No part of this book may be reproduced or transmitted in any form or by any means, electronic or mechanical, including photocopying, recording, or by any information storage and retrieval system without the written permission of the Publisher, except where permitted by law. To request permission and all other inquiries, contact Dreamspinner Press, 382 NE 191st Street #88329, Miami, FL 33179-3899, USA
http://www.dreamspinnerpress.com/

ISBN: 978-1-61581-875-4

Printed in the United States of America
First Edition
January 2012

eBook edition available
eBook ISBN: 978-1-61581-876-1

This book is dedicated to the countless individuals who take their own lives every year. Straight, gay, lesbian, bisexual, or transgendered—every life is important, especially the ones that haven't really had a chance to begin.

CHAPTER ONE

A<small>LEX</small> and Brian half carried me down the sidewalk as I tried to keep up with them and failed miserably. A crappy, fucked-up van sat idling in the driveway. As we got closer, an older guy got out and threw open the side door. It rolled back, making a loud bang as it locked into place. The noise sounded funny, like the ringing of a huge bell, and I started to laugh. My chest hurt, making it hard to laugh and breathe at the same time, so I slowed down. Alex raced ahead of me and jumped into the van, holding his arms out as he turned and knelt on the floor.

"Give him to me—you have to go!" Alex cried and attempted to pull me into the van, but I clung to Brian. I wanted him to go too. I didn't want him to leave me alone again.

"Jamie, honey, I'll be there as soon as I can. Go with Alex. I love you," Brian said as he tried to break my hold. He kissed me on the forehead, letting his lips linger. I knew how he felt—I didn't want to let go either.

"Brian, he can't figure out where we went. We have to go!" Alex jerked me backward, and the pain in my back screamed as I landed on the floor of the van in his arms. I yelled for Brian, but he was already sprinting back toward the house. The old guy told him to go around to the back of the house as he slammed the door shut, cutting off my view of Brian. I didn't understand why Brian couldn't come with us. It made me mad that they hurt me and took him away. I didn't want to go without him.

"I want Brian," I whimpered as Alex scooted back against the opposite wall and pulled me against his thin chest. Scared about what would happen next, I curled up into him and closed my eyes. The van started to move, and I wanted to scream that I didn't understand, but it was Alex. Alex wouldn't hurt me. He wrapped a blanket around the front of my shoulders and then held me tightly against his chest. I could tell he was trying to keep the movement of the vehicle from jostling and jarring me, but I bounced on the floor with each bump and pothole anyway. The drugs dulled the pain in my stomach and back, but I could still feel it.

"It will be okay," he whispered as he held my face against his chest and rubbed the back of my head with his thumb. Gently, he stroked my short hair, and it felt good even though I'd started to lose my buzz. I didn't understand how that could happen when I'd taken so much. Maybe I was dying. I didn't want to die. If it had to happen, I could deal with that, but I wanted to see Brian first. I had to tell him that I loved him and to be happy. I just wanted him to be happy.

"Want Brian.... Don't want to die alone," I murmured against Alex's shirt and felt him tighten his arms around me. Kissing the top of my head, he began to rock back and forth almost imperceptibly.

"I won't let you die, Jamie," he said into my hair as the engine gunned and the van sped up. For the first time since the ride began, I wondered where we were going. Then I wondered if Brian would come, too, and why Alex was holding me instead of him. Thinking about Brian made my heart hurt, but I couldn't understand why.

"I took so much…. He made me take so much…. My chest hurts."

"Leo, maybe we should take him to a hospital," Alex said over my head to the driver. "He said that his chest hurts."

"Is he having trouble breathing?" The man's voice sounded tense, and I looked up to see his eyes flickering to me in the rearview mirror. They were warm and brown like my Brian's eyes. God, I wished Brian were there with me. I missed him so much. Alex put his hand on my chest, and I snuggled closer to him as the van turned. I felt safe sitting there against him. It was a feeling that I didn't quite remember.

"No, I don't think so. His breathing is even, but it's a little faster than mine."

"Okay, just hold on to him until we get to the boarding house. If he starts to feel sick, I put a bucket back there with you. If he starts having trouble breathing, don't keep it a secret. We're almost there."

I zoned out then, the fog taking over my brain. As I shook and swayed from the ride, I wondered if the man was talking about me. I didn't think I'd get sick, but did he really think I'd stop breathing? My stomach prickled even as my head swam. Then the man was talking again, and I felt even more confused.

"Pete, we're almost there. Unlock the back door; I don't want anyone to see us bring him in. I don't know if he'll be able to walk, so we may need your help to get him upstairs…. Yeah, it's bad…. No, Brian and Mike will follow in a little while when it's safe…. Yeah, I have them both with me…. Thanks, Pete." He flipped the phone closed against his leg and put it back into his pocket. Alex shifted underneath me, moving because my elbow was jammed into his ribs.

"Thank you for helping him, Leo," Alex said, and I felt him stroke my cheek as he held me against him. Leo took a deep breath and let it out slowly but didn't turn from the road as he spoke.

"Brian and Mike are my boys. I'd do anything in my power to help them," Leo told him in a low, gruff voice. "But taking him was the easy part. Patching him up, helping him beat his addiction, keeping O'Dell from finding him—those are going to be the real challenges." At the name O'Dell, my whole body tensed, but I felt so confused, and I didn't know why. My breaths came faster, heavier, and my heart, which already felt like it would leap from my chest, sped.

"Jamie, honey, it's okay. We won't let anything happen to you. Please, calm down," Alex whispered and rubbed a hand up and down my back, lightly, as if he was afraid of hurting me. His voice soothed me, but I still couldn't remember why I felt so scared. I was so tired of feeling scared all the time.

"We're here," Leo announced, and we pulled around a rather small and shabby-looking building. The light coming into the van dimmed as we stopped. Leo opened his door and looked around when he got out of the van, then closed the door behind him quickly. When the larger van door opened, he stood there with two guys I didn't recognize. Cool air rushed in from outside, and I suddenly realized I was sweating. Between the heat and being in Alex's arms under a blanket, I felt like the temperature had jumped a hundred degrees in the van. My vision swam, and I shook my head, trying to clear it.

"Come on, hon," Alex said and pushed me toward the door. My legs slid over the edge of the doorway, and I felt my feet land on the ground. My head spun wildly, and I had just enough time to spread my knees before I threw up between my feet. The smell made my stomach lurch like I might be sick again as Alex rubbed my back.

"Better there than on the stairs," Leo said with a sigh. "Okay, get him up. He'll feel better inside where it's cooler." Alex pushed me forward while the two strange men each grabbed one of my arms and hoisted me up. They wrapped an arm around each of their shoulders, and for a few minutes, I was weightless. It took a minute, but I finally got my feet under me when we reached the stairs. Each stair that we climbed felt exactly the same. I put one foot up, and the two men lifted me until I stood solidly on the step. I put my foot on the next stair, and they helped me onto it. By the time we reached the first landing, cold sweat drenched my face, and I felt like I might throw up again.

"Please, just leave me here. I can't…," I started, but they were already lifting me onto the first stair of the second flight. The stairwell shifted, though it could have just been me, and I lost my footing. Alex grabbed my hips and helped to steady me.

"It's okay, kid, we're almost there," the guy on my left said quietly in my ear as we moved up yet another step. My vision may have been tunneling, but that light at the top looked really fucking far away. My heart pounded in my chest, and there just wasn't enough air in the small space for me to breathe. I couldn't get my lungs to pull the air in anymore, and I started to wheeze. The dizziness got worse.

"Fuck, his breathing is getting worse. Hey, Alex, you need to get in front, slide in around Andy, and get his legs." I couldn't tell who had said it. The stairwell had started to spin, but we stopped moving, and I felt them crowd close to me. A small body moved past one of the guys, and my feet were lifted off the stairs. They carried me the rest of the way up and then halfway down a narrow hall. Alex dropped my legs long enough to unlock the door and open it before they took me in. The two guys dropped down on either side of me on the bed and then pushed me back onto something soft. Then the van driver—Leo—put his face right in front of mine, and I tried to focus on it.

"Breathe, Jamie. Slow breaths in and out… come on, kid," he said and took a few deep breaths as if he wanted to show me what to do. I locked my eyes on his and sucked the air into my lungs. As he released his breath, I blew mine out, and then again. After a moment, my vision started to clear, and I could see we were in a small bedroom. It looked completely wrong for the warehouse-style building I thought I saw as we drove up, but I couldn't trust anything right then. Tired, overwhelmed, and fucked up on drugs, I just didn't have the ability to think.

"That's good, just relax." I closed my eyes and kept breathing in and out in synch with Leo. Until his phone rang. My eyes popped open, and I saw him check the display before answering.

"Yeah, babe," came his curt answer as he held the phone up to his ear. "Yeah, he's in the kid's room. We just got him in." Leo paused to listen to the tinny voice on the other end of the line. "He's okay too. Are you guys on your way?" As he paid attention to the conversation, his eyes snapped up to Alex, and he nodded. "Okay, here, kid." I thought he would hand the phone to me, but instead he gave it to Alex.

"Mike?" Alex said quietly. "Yeah, I'm okay. What about you guys? He didn't hurt you, did he?" I couldn't quite focus on what he said after that. My chest hurt, and I still felt so dizzy. Instead, as his mouth continued to move, I tried to breathe.

"Jamie, hon, Brian's coming. They'll be here in a few minutes," Alex said as he handed the phone back to Leo. I felt happy again because Brian would be there soon. I tried to watch Alex as he moved over to the dresser and opened one of the drawers. After a minute of moving things around, he came back with a little computer. "He wants to video chat with his dad when he gets here. He told me to boot it up and try to start the chat," Alex told no one in particular as he opened the computer. I couldn't even care enough to be curious.

"I'm here. Is Brian there yet?" a low voice asked from the computer's speakers. It sounded familiar, but the pain had started to come back, and I didn't feel so good.

"No, Dr. Schreiber, he's on his way. What can I do?" Alex asked, and I looked up to see him staring intently at the screen. That's right. Alex had said Brian wanted to talk to his dad, who was a doctor. I hoped Brian wasn't sick.

"Turn the computer around so I can see him," Richard instructed, and soon I was looking at Brian's father on the screen. "Okay, Alex, I need for you to get his clothes off. Cut them if you have to. I need to be able to see his injuries."

"Leo, do you have a big pair of scissors?" Alex asked, but before Leo could answer, I sat up and pulled my shirt up.

"I can undress myself," I said and hissed when the material stuck to the burn on my stomach. Very carefully, I pulled the cloth away and felt it separate from my skin. When I pulled my shirt over my head, I heard a sharp sound but ignored it because I knew how my body looked. As much as I hated it, Alex had to help me get my jeans off, exposing just how weak I was. I couldn't get the fucking button undone because of the way my hands shook, and it was hard to lift my ass up to pull them down. Everything hurt, and I just had no more strength.

While I reclined back against the pillows, Alex held the laptop over my body with that damn camera on me as he helped Richard with his inspection. After he'd seen my feet, Richard asked me to roll onto my side, which I did with difficulty, and Alex repeated the process with my back.

"Jamie, how did you sustain the burn on your stomach?" Richard asked as Alex held the laptop next to me. My eyes flickered to the angry blisters on my stomach and then to the computer screen.

"Lasagna."

"What does that mean?" Richard asked, sounding confused. My eyes closed again as I tried to think, and then I opened them and held Alex's gaze, willing him to understand.

"He hit you with hot lasagna?" Alex asked with a slight nod, and I nodded back.

"What did you take, and how much?" Richard's voice sounded businesslike as it came through the small computer speakers. I tried to think, to come up with an answer to his question.

"We were at the apartment, and he told me I had to shoot. My stash was gone. It hurt so much. I went in the bedroom to get dressed and found two Es and took those."

"Did you take anything else?" Alex asked gently. "Did Steven give you anything?"

"Yeah, he said I needed to fuck. He gave me coke, a lot of coke."

"How many lines, hon?" Alex stroked my hair as I looked at his face. His eyes looked so scared. I didn't want Alex to be scared.

"Uhm… three, I think. I started to feel sick after two, but he told me not to be a pussy and just do them. But…."

"But what, Jamie?" Richard asked. It helped that he sounded concerned rather than angry. I didn't know if I could explain if he were mad. I didn't want anyone to be mad at me.

"But I don't feel it. I feel confused and tired and sad. Why don't I feel high? Is it because I'm… I'm gonna die?" The question was out before I could stop it. Alex's face went from caring to horrified in an instant.

"No, that's not why you don't feel high." Richard paused like he was trying to decide how to explain. Relieved even though my head was fucking spinning, I tried to focus on his voice. "The cocaine is canceling out the effect of the ecstasy. You have a lot of drugs in your system, and that's dangerous, but it's the type of drugs you took that are making you feel that—" The bedroom door opened, and suddenly Alex jumped off the bed as Brian and Mike hurried into the room.

Brian and Alex charged past each other, and Brian put his hands on either side of my face. Alex hurried over to Mike and threw his arms around Mike's neck.

"Are you alright?" Mike asked Alex and kissed him gently. Alex nodded and pulled Mike to the bed, where they sat at the end.

"Oh God, Jamie," Brian whispered against my neck as he held me. "I thought he was going to kill you. I've never been so scared." The room fell silent, and Brian kissed my forehead before wiping the wetness from his face.

"I'm okay," I told him, trying to make him feel better. I didn't want my Brian to feel bad. I loved him so much.

"Brian, he's not okay," Richard said from the computer, and Brian's head turned to look at the screen. "You need to get him to a hospital."

"Dad, they could call his father. O'Dell could have someone checking the hospitals, looking for him. We can't take him to a hospital unless there's no other way."

Richard and Brian looked at each other over the computer screen, and finally Richard nodded. "Okay, son, but you're doing to have to clean and dress his injuries. Can you do that?"

Brian nodded. "For Jamie, I can do anything."

"I'll send you a list of the supplies you're going to need. But judging from that burn alone, he's going to need stronger pain medication than I can prescribe across state lines." At that, Leo took a step forward. With a deep breath and a look around the room, he spoke.

"I can get you street oxy," he said, while Brian and Mike stared at him. "What? I work with a lot of addicts at the center. You think I don't know any dealers? Besides, oxy isn't Jamie's drug of choice; it won't show up on anyone's radar. Will that do, doc?"

"That wouldn't be my preferred way to do it—you can't count on the strength or quality of illegal drugs—but if you refuse to take him to the hospital, it's the most humane. Brian, you're going to have to debride that burn, and it's going to hurt him badly. He's going to need something." Brian looked at Leo and nodded. Leo pulled out his phone and started to dial as he left the room.

"We can't give him that stuff while he's already got so many drugs in his system, can we?" Brian asked as his hand slid down into mine, linking our fingers together. I loved how that felt. It made me happy.

"No, you can't. When would he have taken it?"

"When did he get to the studio?" Brian asked Mike and Alex, who looked at each other with blank expressions. I didn't even know what time it was then, so I couldn't answer.

"Wait, check your phone. What time did you call Leo? He would have gotten to the studio about ten minutes earlier, and it takes twenty minutes to get to the studio from their building. We can safely say no later than half an hour before you called Leo," Mike explained, and Brian pulled out his cell phone.

"It's been about two hours since he took the drugs," Brian told his father.

"Okay, you're going to need to wait at least four to six hours before you give him anything. You can't debride the burn until he's been given pain meds. I'm going to e-mail you the list of supplies. Someone is going to need to be with Jamie every minute to monitor his breathing and make sure he doesn't choke on his vomit. Do you have someone that can go to a pharmacy and pick these things up for you?" Richard asked, and Brian looked up at Mike.

"Of course I will," Mike said without hesitation.

"I'll go too," Alex offered, but Mike shut him down.

"You will not. If he followed me and Brian, he could be out there. I'm not letting that fucker anywhere near you," he said fiercely, and Alex laid his head on Mike's shoulder as they sat on the bed holding hands.

"Will you stay on with me while I do what you need me to do?" Brian asked, his voice trembling.

"I'll be right here," Richard assured him. "But Brian, if he stops breathing, you have to call an ambulance and you have to tell them exactly what he took. Do you understand? If you don't, his father or this other guy won't matter because he'll die. He has enough drugs in his system to stop his heart." A tear slid down Brian's face as he told Richard he understood.

The computer dinged, and Brian sat up. He did something to the computer and then looked up.

"Okay, my dad sent the list of stuff we're going to need. Mike, can you take my laptop downstairs and hook it up to the printer? Dad, we're going to disconnect until we get what we need. I'll call you when we're ready," Brian said, taking charge. He said goodbye to his father before handing the laptop to Mike. Mike, Alex, and the other two guys from earlier all left together. Leo hadn't returned, so Brian and I were alone. He continued to sit next to me on the bed, holding my hand. I rested my head on his shoulder just to be closer to him.

"No matter what happens, promise me you won't ever forget," I told him, and he squeezed me tighter, making me wince. If there really was a chance that I could die, I had to make sure he knew that. I didn't want him to wonder how I felt—ever. I loved him so much.

"I'm not going to let you die, Jamie." The pain in Brian's voice told me that he was just as scared as I was. He could say the words all he wanted, but he had no more control over the situation than I did.

"I'm so tired," I said and closed my eyes. Brian shifted on the bed, and after a minute, I heard him talking, but it wasn't to me.

"Dad, can he sleep?" I opened my eyes, blinking slowly, and saw him on the phone. "I won't leave him. I'll sit right here with my hand on his chest." Brian's voice cracked, and the bad feeling came back. I had made Brian sad. "Thanks, Dad. I'll text you and check in every hour.... Yes."

"Honey, Dad says you can sleep if you want to," Brian whispered, and a chuckle bubbled up from my chest.

"What?" Brian asked and tilted my face up so that I was looking at him. His answering smile was angelic, and I moved my face closer to kiss him.

"You called me 'honey'... I like that," I told him with another short laugh.

"You get through this, and I'll call you whatever you want, sweetheart," he said, suddenly serious. He stroked my face lightly, and I scooted down a little in the bed to rest. Laying my head on his hip, I felt him playing with my hair.

"I love you," I told him but fell asleep before I heard his reply.

CHAPTER TWO

MY HEAD fucking pounded, and I tried not to open my eyes even though the room was dark and cool. I had no idea if it was really late or really early, but I had the feeling that I'd slept for a very long time. The fact that Steven hadn't woken me felt ominous. A weight pressed on my chest, but it was almost comforting, like when my mom used to put her hand on my forehead if I had a fever. As I struggled for consciousness, I tried to think of the last thing I remembered. We were getting ready to go to the shoot, and I took some E, but I couldn't remember going to the studio or being in a scene.

"Jamie, honey, are you awake?"

My eyes burned as I opened them. The low light coming in from behind faded denim curtains allowed me to see the small bedroom where I lay. A dresser sat opposite the bed with that stupid stuffed pink poodle that Alex loved so much standing guard on top. Pop art and posters covered the walls—pop art and posters that I was used to seeing in Alex's apartment. I had no idea what the fuck was happening. Why was Alex's stuff scattered around this tiny closet of a bedroom?

"Hi, babe," Brian said, and I looked down to see that the weight on my chest was his hand. My gaze followed his hand to his arm up to his face. He smiled at me, radiating every bit of the sweetness and love that I'd come to expect when he looked at me. I smiled back, the warmth spreading through my chest as my heart started to race.

Then panic hit me like a fucking freight train.

I was in a room full of Alex's stuff that wasn't Alex's bedroom. Brian was sitting next to me on the bed looking for all the world like nothing was wrong. I had no memory of how I got to wherever I was.

Jesus, they fucking took me. They managed to take me from Steven. Holy Goddamn Christ, he's going to kill us all.

Brian's face fell as he watched my changing expressions.

"What the hell did you do, Brian?" I whispered, horrified by what was going to happen to him, to Alex, and to me when Steven found me. He would find me. I had no illusions about that. I sat up, my head spun, and my face broke out in a cold sweat. A bucket was shoved into my hands, and I dry heaved into it.

"Jamie, it's okay… you're safe now," Brian assured me as he ran a hand lightly up and down my back. I took a few deep breaths. Jesus, Brian had always been a smart guy—how could he be so stupid?

"What the fuck did you do?" I yelled, and Brian flinched. He sat staring wide-eyed at me while the panic rose from my chest up into my throat, nearly strangling me. The pain radiating through my body, while almost blinding, took a back seat to the clusterfuck in front of me. That pain would be nothing compared to what we were all in for when Steven found me.

"I couldn't leave you with him, Jamie. I couldn't," Brian whispered, and the choking sound of his voice left a pain in my chest that had nothing to do with my injuries. I slid over to the edge of the bed and threw my legs over the side. Brian put a hand on my shoulder and tried to stop me from getting up. "You need to rest. Dad said—"

"Oh Christ, your father is here too?" I asked, not bothering to mask my sarcasm. "Anyone else know I'm here? Did you maybe put up a billboard?" He didn't answer, and I looked up to see that fucking kicked puppy expression he'd worn at the studio when I did my best to stay away from him. It made me even angrier. As I tried to stand up, Brian pulled out a cell phone and typed on it.

"No, my dad assessed your injuries using my webcam and told us to let the *fuck-ton* of drugs in your system work their way out before we helped you. He thought that the sheer amount of shit you'd taken might stop your heart, but it didn't," he told me in a hollow voice as I finally succeeded in getting to my feet. It felt like my body just didn't work right. I was tired, hurting, and scared.

"Where are we? Why is all of Alex's stuff in this room?" I asked, and before he could answer, the door opened. Alex came in, followed by Mike, Emilio, Leo, and two guys I didn't know. The room was suddenly packed with bodies, and I started to feel claustrophobic. It got hard to breathe, and I sat back down on the bed.

"Jamie, oh hon, we've been so worried," Alex said and climbed onto the bed next to me, pulling me into his arms. He was warm and smelled like fruit and sweat and sunshine. To have him there felt normal, and I could breathe again. Looking into his face reminded me of Steven's threat.

"He's going to hurt you, Alex. He's going to hurt all of them, but you worst of all. How could you let them do this?" I whispered, burying my face in his neck. "I'm not worth it."

"When he pulled you out after he got into it with Mike, we thought he was going to kill you. We started getting things ready, and when he brought you to the studio and you were so…. Oh God, Jamie, we had to do something," Alex said, rubbing his hand lightly up and down my back. I sat there, ignoring the rest of the room as I felt his comfort, surrounded by the smell of that fruity body wash he used, and tried to decide what to do.

"Where are we?"

"We're at the boarding house where Mike lives, and now where I live," he whispered back. I sat up and searched his face.

"You gave up your apartment to move in here? Where's the rest of your stuff? It can't all fit in this tiny room." My voice shook as I asked. He had given up his life and his freedom to move into a fucking closet, and it was my fault.

"A lot of my stuff is in storage upstairs, and some of it I lent to Brian. He's been staying in this room while we get things ready. I've been staying in Mike's room. I mean, yes, I gave up my apartment, but I actually like it here, Jamie. I have friends here, and I'm not alone all the time. The rent is cheaper, so Mike and Leo are going to help me set up some investments. I won't be living from paycheck to paycheck anymore. The best part is, I get to be here with Mike," he said and held out his hand. Mike took a step forward and held it.

"So, wait, you guys are…." I trailed off, letting him pick up on my meaning.

"We're seeing where things go. So far, we like where they're going," Alex said with a laugh. "And Brian got this cute little apartment for the two of you. You should see it. He even got a big bed that one of Leo's friends was selling." Then, a little lower, more seriously, he said, "He's not going to find you, Jamie."

I nodded because I didn't want to disillusion him. Alex had always been an idealist. He always thought the best of people until they proved him wrong. Somehow, they usually did. I'd let him think that they'd charged in on their little white horses and saved me, at least for right then, until I decided what to do.

"So, what happens now?" I asked the room at large. Alex looked at Mike, who looked at Leo, who turned to Brian. I followed the exchange and saw that Brian appeared uncomfortable. "What?"

"According to my dad, the drugs would have worked themselves out of your system. We need to give you some pain pills that Leo has and then take care of your injuries." I couldn't deny that my body hurt and that I needed some antibiotics. A couple of E wouldn't hurt either, but I doubted that I'd get that with Brian.

"That doesn't sound so bad," I said and fell back against the pillows next to where Brian sat on the bed.

"My dad said we need to cut the top layer of dead skin off of your burn, Jamie. It's going to hurt, a lot. That's why we need the pain pills. Then we can clean and dress the cuts and maybe put an ice pack on your eye."

"Oh...." I replied and closed my eyes. That didn't sound pleasant at all. No one spoke, and the silence hung heavy in the overfilled room. Finally, Leo asked Brian where he wanted to set up.

"I think he'll be more comfortable on the bed—my dad said that was okay. Alex, babe, can you hand me my laptop? I need to get my dad on the webcam."

My breathing accelerated. It's not that I really feared pain. God knows I had gotten used to it. Not knowing exactly what was going to happen, that scared me. *What if it hurt worse than I could handle? What if Brian cut something he wasn't supposed to? What if I got some kind of infection? What if Brian found something* he *couldn't handle?* A million other "what if" questions ran through my head as Mike picked up a couple of pharmacy bags from the floor, and the two guys I didn't know cleared out of the room.

"Em, I'm going to need some towels and washrags," Brian said as he worked on the computer. "Mike, can you and Alex put the card table up over there and set out that stuff?"

Alex unfolded the legs on the big square table, pushed it back against the wall, and then he and Mike started pulling prescription bottles, gauze, peroxide, and about a dozen other packages out of the bags and setting them on the table in no discernable order.

"Hi, Dad," Brian said, bringing my attention back to him and to the computer. I saw Richard on the screen.

"Hi, son," he said with a grim smile, and then he looked at me. "Jamie, you're looking better. How do you feel?" Rubbing the back of my neck, I thought about my answer and decided just to tell him the truth.

"I'm hurting, I have a headache, and I'm scared," I told him as I kept my eyes on the screen to avoid looking at Brian.

"You would be much better off going to a hospital—"

"I can't go to a hospital. They'd either call Steven or my parents, and I don't particularly want either of them deciding what happens to me." Out of the corner of my eye, I saw Brian nod.

"Okay, Brian, do you have everything I told you to get?" I heard the heavy disapproving sigh in Richard's voice, but I refused to go to a hospital. If my parents found out where I was, they would put me back in the Center. If Steven found me, he'd do so much worse.

"Yeah, Dad, and Leo has the oxy."

Great, as if I needed something else to add to my growing addiction. But deep down, I couldn't wait to feel numb. I didn't want to hurt anymore, and I certainly didn't want to think anymore. Sick of worrying and feeling scared all the time, I would welcome the oblivion of the drugs just as I always did.

"Let's start with the smaller cuts and scrapes first; then he won't have to move once the burn is dressed," Richard instructed from the small screen. Brian opened a box of latex gloves and put on a pair.

"Jamie, can you lay on your side?" Brian asked, and I tried to roll onto my side so that my back faced him, but pain seared through my stomach and back. I flinched and whimpered around the stabbing burn. "Okay, let's try something else. Can you sit up for me?" Very carefully, I scooted back over to the edge of the bed, and Emilio helped me to sit up. I was sweating from the pain and the exertion by the time he released me.

My feet rested on something soft and fluffy, so I looked down and saw Alex's bright purple rug. The light blanket around me was pulled away from my back, and I heard Brian ask for the peroxide. Leo handed me two white pills and a glass of milk. When I asked, he told me that the milk would be better on my stomach since I hadn't eaten in hours. I couldn't remember the last time I'd eaten but didn't feel hungry in any case.

I felt pressure on my back, as if Brian held something there, and then the cold rushing of peroxide over my skin. The bubbling sting caused me to jerk, but he and Emilio continued to clean the cut. It felt like they were working on the spot where the dinner plate had sliced my back. I couldn't see, so I didn't know how big it was, but it had bled like crazy all over the white floor.

"Hand me those butterfly bandages, Em…. Yeah, open them up," Brian said, and I tried to hold as still as I could. Leo stood by the door watching, while Mike and Alex sat on the floor next to the bed. It felt…

reassuring to have them all there with me. Being surrounded by people who cared made me relax a bit.

Once the cut was closed, Brian cleaned about half a dozen other spots on my back with the rag and peroxide but didn't put bandages on them. Richard said they would heal better if he kept them exposed to the open air.

"Okay, Brian, you're going to have to wash the burn and the surrounding skin with a little soap and water. You need to make sure that the area is as sterile as you can get it," Richard said, and Alex stood up from where he had been sitting against Mike.

"I'll get you some soap and water," he said as he walked over to the dresser and grabbed a turquoise tote with a plastic handle. Reaching in, he pulled out body wash, tossed it to Mike, and left the room. Brian pushed me back so that I reclined on a single pillow, almost flat on the small bed. The cuts on my back were nothing, and I started to get nervous about how bad the procedure would hurt. It was a few minutes before I realized that the pain in my body had almost gone. The pills I'd taken were starting to kick in.

Alex came back in carrying two plastic bowls, covered with lids, on a cookie sheet.

"Tea service?" Mike asked, and I could hear the laughter in his voice.

"Shut up. I was afraid I'd spill the water on the stairs," Alex said with a pout. I felt the tray bump my hip as he set it on the bed. Brian grabbed Alex's hand before he could move back to his place on the floor.

"Will you sit up there by the head of the bed and talk to him? We need for him to stay calm while I do this," Brian whispered, but his voice was loud enough that I could still hear him. It never failed to amaze me how Brian always put others first, no matter what he had to do.

"Brian?" I asked, my head starting to feel a little fuzzy from the oxy.

"Yeah, babe?" His hands were gentle as he began to wash my stomach. The tropical scent of Alex's body wash made me smile. Brian smiled back.

"I'm sorry that I yelled at you." *I love you, and it will kill me if he hurts you. You are everything to me.*

"It's okay," he said with a shrug. I think he was trying to sound casual, but the tension in his face and his posture told a different story. It occurred to me that he didn't want to argue about anything while he was trying to keep me calm enough to take care of the burn. So, rather than trying to press the issue any further, I simply thanked him for taking care of me.

He tossed the soapy rag back into the first bowl and picked up a clean rag from the pile that Emilio had brought.

"I will always be here to take care of you," he whispered and kissed my forehead. Using slow strokes, he started to rinse the soap off my skin, and I felt a warm glow deep inside me that had nothing to do with the drugs. Alex moved a small collapsible chair next to the bed and sat down. The chair looked like the kind we used to use when we went camping.

"So, what's new?" Alex asked in a lispy, energetic, effeminate voice, and I couldn't help it—I laughed. With the drugs in my system to relax me, it sounded more like a giggle than a laugh in my head. He reached over and took my hand. "O-M-G," he said, sounding excited. "Jamie, I met the hottest guy. His name is Mike, and he just... God."

Alex signed theatrically, and I laughed again. In a stage whisper, he continued, "He has the biggest dick. It's truly a work of art."

"I am still here," Mike said wryly from the floor on the other side of the bed.

"Shh…," Alex said. "I'm telling a story here, babe."

Mike, Brian, and Emilio all laughed, and Brian tossed the rag he'd used to rinse my skin back into the bowl. He handed the tray to Em, who took it out of the room.

"Anywhoo, we were in New Orleans, which is fabulous by the way. If you ever have a chance to go, you totally should." Alex's free hand was waving in the air as he continued to talk animatedly about spending the week in New Orleans as if I hadn't been there with them. I never could understand what Brandon and some of the other guys had against Alex, because he was an amazing person.

"So, the friend that I flew down with kind of ditched me when we got to the hotel and took off with another guy," Alex said and rolled his eyes. I giggled again, and Brian chuckled as he draped some kind of medical paper over my bare abdomen.

"Brian, you just need to cover the area surrounding the burn to keep it sterile. Make sure that you can see all of the affected area," Richard said quietly from the computer, and I'd nearly forgotten that he was still watching. I wondered how he was going to feel about listening to Alex's account of his time with Mike, but I could focus on only so many things at one time, so I concentrated on Alex's voice and nothing else as Em walked back into the room.

"But this guy that I roomed with instead, Jamie… God, he was so hot. That first night, we were getting ready for bed. It had been such a long day that I was almost asleep when he came out of the bathroom after his shower, but wow. He walked out in just a towel, and I swear I nearly creamed my superhero jammie bottoms!"

"Jesus Christ," Mike muttered from the floor with a barely concealed laugh. The bottom of the bed dipped, and I glanced over to see that Mike had moved up onto the bed near my feet. The look he gave Alex was indulgent but sweet, as if there were no one else in the world he'd rather see. I saw that look often, in Brian's eyes.

"Okay, now take out the sterile scissors and tweezers. You need to remove as much of the damaged skin as you can, and then treat the burn with the Silvadene." Richard's voice came again from the small speakers, and Alex stroked my hair as he continued to talk to me in that same cheery tone.

"So, that next night, we went out dancing. Emilio went too," Alex said with a smile over at Emilio, who assisted Brian by carefully removing the medical supplies from their packages with gloved hands. Alex's voice dropped to a conspiratorial whisper, "Then he ran off with a hot Bayou boy, and we didn't see him again." I looked over at Emilio, who smiled cheekily and continued with his work.

"And what did you guys do?" I asked Alex, not too interested in the answer but more to distract myself from the sight of Brian with those little scissors over my stomach.

"We were on the dance floor, and Mike was dancing behind me. He slid his fingers up under my shirt and moved against me. It wasn't anything aggressive, just light and fun. But, God, Jamie, I was so turned on, I almost came right there on the dance floor!" Alex finished in a squeal, and I felt something hard and sharp hit my chest.

"Ow!" I whimpered and rubbed my chest under the paper drapes. "What the hell?"

"Sorry, I'm sorry," Brian murmured and quickly snatched the scissors from where they'd fallen on my chest. I looked up at him and noticed that his face was bright red; a flush had crept over his forehead, his cheeks, and even his neck. I wondered if he'd blushed so deeply because of Alex telling his story where Richard could hear, but then he hadn't acted like that when Alex talked about Mike coming out of the shower. Mike snorted, and it felt like I was missing a joke. I wanted to ask one of them about it, but then those scissors moved toward my stomach. I tensed all over, all thoughts of Brian's embarrassment forgotten.

"S-so, what do you like about him?" I asked as my body broke out in a cold sweat in the warm room.

"Close your eyes, Jamie," Alex whispered as he took my hand. "It will be over soon, hon." Not wanting to see what cutting away my skin would uncover, I did as he suggested. Brian's hands were steady, and I felt an almost rhythmic pinch and pull. I'm sure my imagination was worse than the reality of it, but in my mind's eye, I saw him pulling my skin up with the tweezers. Then a slight tearing as he started to cut into the damaged area. My breathing accelerated, and it felt like someone had sucked the air from the room. The pain seeped in, even around the barrier of the painkillers.

"I like that he listens to me," Alex said, his voice softer as he switched from his sexual relationship with Mike to their emotional connection. Making an effort to put the medical stuff out of my mind, I was startled to hear the vulnerability in Alex's voice. "I like that he really sees me. I'm not just a body for him to get off on, or a guy to call when he gets an itch. With him, I can be Alex, and that's okay."

The more damaged skin Brian cut away, the worse the pain seemed to become, until I could no longer stop myself from shifting on the bed to get away from it.

"Jamie, I'm almost done." Brian's tension was evident in the tightness of his voice. "Baby, you need to lay still."

I knew I needed to stay still, but the pain was so intense that I couldn't. Writhing on the bed, I heard Brian's gasp just as the cold edge of the scissors touched the inside of the burn, and I screamed.

"Mike!" Brian yelled above my scream, and I felt two strong arms holding my chest to the bed. Again, I tried to stay still, but it was almost as if my body had a mind of its own, as if it wanted to get away from the pain no matter what my brain said.

"Stop! Please stop… it hurts!" I cried even as Alex joined Mike in holding me still. The fire that consumed my stomach continued to rage. It felt like my skin was melting. When I opened my eyes, I found Brian, his face covered in tears as he worked. Finally, with one last pull, he handed something I couldn't see to Emilio. And then it felt like Steven was burning me with the welding torch he kept in the basement, and I screamed again, begging him to stop hurting me. I told him I'd do anything… anything, please just make it stop. My throat was hoarse, and pain ripped through every part of me.

"The Silvadene is on the bandage—hand me some strips from the tape!" Brian yelled. I heard terrible ripping noises, as if someone were pulling huge chunks of my flesh from my body. Then a pain like I'd never known tore across my skin as he pressed something hard against my stomach.

Finally, fate showed me a moment of compassion, and I lost consciousness.

CHAPTER THREE

WHEN I woke, panic enveloped me in the pitch-black room. After panic came the pain. Sharp, bright spots of fire peppered my arms and legs, but my stomach was an inferno. As I squirmed on the bed and tried to find that one sweet spot, that one position that would make the pain lessen even a little, I heard a quiet whimper. My eyes began to adjust to the lack of light, and I looked around. After a moment, I remembered that I was in Alex's new little bedroom at the boarding house.

I turned on his bedside lamp, the Tiffany-style glass lamp he'd stolen from his house as a reminder of his mother. The room burst with faded blue light, and I tried not to move as I scanned the room for the source of the noise.

"Stop… please don't hurt him," Brian's voice shook as he begged, and my stomach screamed in protest as I leaned over the side of the bed to find him curled up on the floor. He kicked out, and I tried to reach down to shake him awake, but the pain was just too much.

"Brian," I said firmly over the side, willing him to wake. He whimpered again in his sleep, like a wounded dog. The tension and fear in his face tugged at my heart. I couldn't just let him stay in that dream. Too many nights he'd woken frightened and alone because I wasn't there. I wouldn't let that happen if I could help it.

"Brian," I said, louder that time, and looked around for something to prod him with, but there was nothing within reach.

"Goddamn fuck!" I cried as I rolled onto my side, and pain lanced through my body. Reaching down, I smacked Brian's arm once, and sweat beaded my forehead when I fell on my back against the pillow. Tears of pain welled in my eyes and then fell unobstructed. But by the grace of God, Brian sat straight up, his head now visible as I lay panting.

"Oh my God, are you okay?" Brian asked as he looked over to see me clutching my stomach and rocking gently back and forth. He sat on the floor, disoriented for several seconds, as his hand rested on my arm.

"You were having a nightmare…," I panted, "…couldn't wake you up." He groaned as he lifted himself off the hard floor where he had been sleeping, and I scooted over the best I could as he climbed in bed with me. He lay on his side with his head on my shoulder. As small as the bed was, he must have been clinging to the edge.

"I'm sorry," he whispered and kissed my sweaty forehead. Pushing the damp hair away, he let his lips rest against my temple.

"Why were you lying on the floor, anyway?" I tried to change the subject from the horrible pain and focus on something else. My breathing still felt labored, and a bead of sweat rolled down my cheek.

"I didn't want to bother you while you were sleeping, but I couldn't make myself leave," he whispered. Running his fingers up and down my arm lightly, he kept touching me, and the feeling of his skin on mine calmed me. "I didn't want you to wake up alone."

I lifted the arm closest to him and wrapped it around his shoulders.

"Wait." He rolled off the bed quickly, careful not to jostle me, and left the room. For several minutes, I stared at the closed door and wondered where he'd gone. I didn't hear anything outside of the room and felt a little disoriented. In Steven's apartment, we could usually hear street traffic or noise from the other apartments. I looked over at the bedside clock and saw that it was just past three in the morning. That might also have something to do with the lack of noise.

The door opened, and Brian came in with a mug. Setting it on the side table, he closed the door quietly behind him and sat on the edge of the bed.

"Do you need help sitting up?"

I honestly didn't know if I did or not, but I found that scooting up in the bed was easier on my injuries than trying to roll over. Propping myself on the pillows, however, caused some considerable pain.

"I have some more pain pills for you, and Dad wants you to take them with this. It's just a cup of hot soup," he explained and handed me the pills. I snatched them out of his hand and dropped them into my mouth, which felt like the Sahara at that moment. My hands trembled when I took the mug of soup, and I spilled a little of the broth on my naked chest in my haste, singeing a few of the hairs there.

"Hey, take it slow," Brian warned, but I wanted to get the pills down. Pain radiated through my body, and I was desperate to feel that numbness again. The hard, chalk-like pellets finally passed the lump in my throat and slid down into my stomach. With a desperate sigh of relief, I tried to hand the mug back to Brian, but he refused to take it.

"You need to drink all of that." His voice was firm but kind as he pushed the mug gently back toward my lips. "Dad wants you to drink lots of clear liquids, and then when you're up to it, start with some soft food." Brian leaned down and kissed my lips lightly. His whisper was conspiratorial against my ear, and I failed to suppress a shiver.

"If you drink that soup and keep it down, I'll make you a grilled cheese and some tomato soup later for lunch."

"I used to love grilled cheese and tomato soup. I don't think I've had it in years." The sadness that I heard in my own confession startled me. Given what we were all facing, being sentimental over a sandwich was just fucking ridiculous. I took a drink of broth to give myself a reason to shut the hell up.

When I finished with the mug, Brian set it on the table next to the bed and then stood up. Panic swelled in my throat, making it hard to breathe. I grabbed his hand before I could stop myself, and he looked down at me. My heart pounded in my chest, and for a minute, I couldn't even make myself speak.

"Jamie?"

"Where are you going?" My voice shook, and I know I sounded near tears. I had no explanation for the panic, but deep in my soul, I just *knew* if he walked out that door, I'd never see him again. Steven would be out in the hall, or downstairs waiting for Brian. He would take Brian and torture him, pulling his flesh away from his bones with a utility knife. I could almost hear Brian screaming even over the sounds of my ragged breathing.

"I was just going to lie down on the couch down—"

"Stay with me? Please?" I pleaded and held back a grimace at the fire in my belly when I rolled over to give him room on the bed. Brian's face was almost alarmed when he pulled off his T-shirt and climbed in bed behind me. His strong arm wrapped around my chest, careful not to go any lower and touch the bandages on my abdomen. I felt his hand settle over my heart, and finally, I could take a full breath.

"He's not going to find you, Jamie. I won't let him hurt you ever again," Brian whispered in my ear. I turned my head slightly, and he lifted up onto an elbow so that he could see my face.

"It's not me I'm worried about him hurting," I whispered, and Brian dipped his head, capturing my lips carefully, as if I might break.

Then he pulled me back against his broad chest and held me until I fell asleep. The last thing I remembered was that I'd never felt so safe.

THE sun crept in through the window as I woke. My body and my head both ached from the pain and stress of the previous day. An arm tightened its hold around my chest, and for just a moment, I allowed myself to smile. One of the greatest joys of my life those last few months in Alabama had been waking up in Brian's arms. I had loved the way he smelled, the way he would nuzzle against my skin, still half caught in his dreams, and most of all the way he would whisper my name as if it were a promise.

"Mmm… Jamie." Brian's whisper against my skin made me shiver. He tightened his hold further and scooted his body closer on the small bed. His morning wood pressed against my ass, and even through the pain, I felt a flare of heat. I savored the feeling of his hand on my chest and his breath against my neck for several minutes before I rolled carefully onto my back and looked up at him. Almost as if I were made of glass, he pressed his lips against mine with the gentlest of touches. His nose bumped lightly against my cheek as his mouth slanted over mine, moving in a natural, timeless rhythm. The love that I held deep in my heart filled my chest, and I couldn't breathe for the intensity of it.

It didn't matter that neither of us hadn't brushed, that the bed was too small, or even that my body ached from the beatings I'd endured. In that moment, all that mattered was the comfort I found in him. With Brian, I felt like just maybe everything could be okay again.

Brian moved a little closer, his leg wrapping around mine as his arms cradled me in his protective hold. I felt his cock pressed against my hip, so I reached down between us and stroked him lightly as we lay entwined in nothing but our briefs. His warm, naked skin against mine was like a salve on my broken soul, and I clung to him. He had risked so much, done so much for me, and I had no way to show him how thankful I was for it.

Or… maybe, I did.

Sliding my hand down further between us, I rubbed his erection through the thin briefs. I liked the way the soft cotton felt on my fingers, and the damp spot made his desire clear. The kiss intensified with electrified meetings of our lips, tongues, and teeth.

"I-I can't fuck yet, but I can suck you," I whispered against his mouth. When he started to protest, I kissed him again to stop it. "You've done so much for me. It's the least I can—"

He sat up and looked at me as if he'd never seen me before.

"You think I helped you so that you would suck me off? Is that really how little you think of me?" Brian pulled away from me and climbed out of bed with a speed I certainly wouldn't have been capable of right then. Before I could call him back, he'd grabbed his jeans and walked out of the small room. I just stared after him as the aches in my back, my stomach, and now my chest brought tears to my eyes. That hadn't been what I'd meant at all. I knew exactly why he'd helped me… because he loved me. All I'd wanted to do was show him that I loved him and that I appreciated him. But I fucked it up—just like I fucked up everything else in my life. I felt cold as I stared at the ceiling, not really seeing it.

After a few minutes, I couldn't stand the silence anymore. I couldn't stand being alone or knowing that Brian was upset. I picked up my T-shirt from where it had landed on a small chair next to the bed. Carefully, I slid over to the edge of the bed and gritted my teeth as I let my feet dangle over the side. It was a minute or two before my toes touched the plush rug, signaling that they were finally on the floor. Pain shot through my stomach and chest when I tried to sit up on the side of the bed. I couldn't stop the low cry as I wrapped my arm around myself in a futile attempt to curb the agony. Taking a deep breath, I used my other arm to push until I was upright. With a whimper and a sharp pain in my back, I stood. My skin stretched and pinched when I pulled the T-shirt over my head. It took a surprisingly large number of tiny steps for me to reach the door to the bedroom, and each one sent pinpricks of fire to my torso.

The stairs were worse.

I leaned against the railing, forcing it to take as much of my weight as I could, and slid against the wall as I moved from one step to the next. The cuts on my back burned as they slid against the worn drywall through my shirt. I inched my way down as I kept my back to the wall. It was a slow, agonizing trip, and the concrete steps were ice cold under my bare feet. My pants were still upstairs somewhere, but it didn't matter.

The door on the landing below burst open, and two bodies came through before it banged shut again. The first body slammed against the opposite wall with the second body right on top of it. I wanted to yell for someone to help until I saw that they weren't exactly fighting.

"God, you smell good," Mike murmured against Alex's neck as he lifted him. Alex wrapped his legs around Mike's waist, both of them oblivious to the fact that I stood just feet from them. I thought about speaking up, but something in the way they were kissing held me back.

When I was with Steven, I missed kissing like that. Two souls intertwined, connected by lips, love, and need. In our tree house, even in New Orleans, Brian and I had spent hours kissing. Mike rolled his hips between Alex's legs, pressing him harder against the wall. Alex's head fell back, and he moaned as Mike's mouth moved to his neck. He was pulling Mike's shirt up his back in an effort to take it off when he spotted me.

"Jamie!" he said in surprise.

"Hey, at least get the name right," Mike said as he pulled back. When he noticed that Alex was looking over his shoulder, he turned slightly, not releasing his hold on Alex, and saw me standing there.

"Mike, put me down. He needs help," Alex said, pushing away from the wall, impatient to get to me.

"Ah, hell," Mike said, bending his knees and easing Alex back to the ground. Alex immediately rushed to my side and put one of my arms around his shoulders. He helped me descend the last few stairs, and I sat down on the cold concrete to rest.

"Why are you in the stairwell? Why aren't you in bed? What's wrong?" A slow and steady hand stroking my back accompanied Alex's rapid-fire questions. My head fell into my hands, and I closed my eyes.

"Brian and I had a misunderstanding. I wanted to come down and see him," I explained and saw Mike tense. The cold seeping through my briefs started to make my back ache, and I wondered if maybe coming downstairs wasn't such a great idea. Brian would have come back up eventually, or I could have asked someone to get him. My impulsiveness just continued to get me into trouble.

"What the hell did you do this time?" Sarcasm dripped from each word, and I slid my hands up behind my neck, linked my fingers, and continued to stare at the ground. I didn't want to get into it with Mike, not then.

The door opened, and I looked up to see Brian standing there with a grilled cheese sandwich, a bowl, and a can of soda balanced on a cookie sheet. He stopped short when he saw us, but he didn't drop his makeshift tray.

"Jamie, what are you doing out of bed?" Brian set the tray on the stairs next to me and put his hand on the side of my face. I leaned into the touch, thankful that he didn't seem angry anymore.

"I came down to apologize," I said with my eyes trained on the floor beneath my feet because I didn't want to see the disappointment and hurt in his face again. Mike made a scathing noise, and my already frayed nerves just snapped. I was fucking sick of his shit.

"What the fuck is your problem?" I asked and struggled to get to my feet. Alex held me as I stood up, and Brian got between us. It was stupid to get into it with Mike because I was in no shape to defend myself, but the way he kept trying to come between Brian and me just pissed me off.

"I'm sick of seeing you hurt them," Mike growled back at me, pushing Brian a little in his anger. His normally fair complexion flushed as he glared over Brian's shoulder. Alex wrapped his thin arms around my chest, holding me back against him with as much strength as he could find.

"Mike, he's not hurting me," Alex said quietly.

"Really, Alex? Where's Allie?" Mike asked, but his voice had softened, and I felt Alex stiffen behind me. I didn't understand what he meant.

"Mike, that's not fair." The hitch in Alex's voice made me think I'd missed something vital.

"Who's Allie?" I asked over my shoulder, but Alex didn't answer.

"Allie was a kitten Alex found in the alley behind his building just after we got back from New Orleans. He'd taken it to the vet, got a litter box and collar, and fallen in love with the little thing. Then he had to get rid of her when he gave up his apartment to move in here because of you!"

"Mike—" Alex started, but Mike held up a hand.

"You hurt Brian every single day. Do you notice how much weight he's lost? I do. I see it whenever I look at him. You're hurting two guys I love, and I'm not going to—" Mike stopped talking at the squeak that came from Alex behind me. We all turned to look at Alex, whose face had lit up like Christmas morning. He looked at Mike with so much affection and tenderness that I felt like an intruder.

"You love me?" Normally Alex was larger than life, but his voice had gotten very small and unsure as he asked the question. Mike relaxed a little as he gazed back into Alex's face. The fight seemed to have left him as he realized what he'd just admitted. He nodded, and suddenly the arms around me disappeared. I staggered as Alex launched himself at Mike. Mike's back hit the wall just as Brian wrapped his arm around my waist to steady me.

"Take me upstairs," Alex murmured between heated kisses. His anger forgotten for the moment, Mike took Alex's hand and led him past Brian and me. Avoiding the tray of food getting cold on the stairs, he pulled Alex up to the third floor. They disappeared from view with a giggle and a bang as the door closed.

Brian kissed my forehead as I leaned into him. I didn't care about the food, or about Mike and Alex—all I wanted was Brian. Shivering against the cool air of the stairwell and the cold concrete under my bare feet, I burrowed closer into Brian's warmth. He wrapped both his arms around me, and I sighed against his shoulder.

"Let's get you back upstairs. I made you some lunch," he whispered and pulled away.

"No way am I going upstairs with those two fucking in the next room," I said. "Can't we just stay down here somewhere?" I hadn't been in any part of the building except Alex's room upstairs. Since Brian had made food, though, I figured there must be a kitchen of some sort on the other side of that door. Even if we just sat at a dining room table, anything would be better than listening to Mike's bedframe slamming against the wall as he pounded Alex into the mattress.

"Yeah, we can hang out down here in the common room," Brian said as he reached down to grab the tray of food. "Sit here for just a second, and I'll put this tray in there first. I don't want anyone to step on it if they come downstairs."

I leaned against the wall as he opened the door and carried the tray through. It really was just a matter of seconds before he was back and helping me up. The comfortable room on the other side of the door surprised me. I barely remembered arriving at the building and coming up the stairs, but I had gotten the sense that it was more industrial than residential.

This room looked more like a frat house than an office, however. A pool table, a couch, a few mismatched chairs, and a TV took up most of the room. The stuff looked second-hand, but it was more of a home than any place I'd seen in the last few years. I wondered what it would be like to live there with Brian and Alex, somewhere I actually belonged. Then I reminded myself that it was only temporary. Soon, Steven would find me, and my vacation into normalcy would be all over.

"Here, sit by the table," Brian said, helping me to sit on the couch near the tray of food. "I'm going to run upstairs and get you a blanket." I wanted to argue with him, to keep him there with me, but I was cold, and a blanket sounded great. He kissed me gently and then headed for the door.

I looked around again and saw that there was a small kitchen off the main room and another door labeled "Manager" nearby. Too tired to worry about anything else, I grabbed the grilled cheese sandwich from the plate and took a bite. It was a work of golden-fried art wrapped around a thick layer of gooey cheese. If I'd died the day before, then I was surely in heaven.

By the time Brian returned with the blanket, I'd already finished the sandwich and was working on the tomato soup. Even though it had been made from concentrated goop in a can, there was something about it that soothed my soul. It warmed me from the inside, and I felt so much better after I'd finished. Brian carried the blanket to the far end of the couch and sat down. Satisfied that I'd eaten everything, he scooted back against the side of the couch and opened his arms. I crawled into them greedily and rested against his chest as he covered us with the blanket.

"I'm sorry I overreacted earlier," he murmured against my ear. I turned my head to kiss him softly.

"I didn't mean it like that. I just… I didn't know how to thank you for everything that you've done for me. I don't deserve it, but I'm so grateful." Nestling into the crook of his neck, I rested my body against his and delighted in the feeling of his arms around me and his love surrounding me.

"You do deserve it. I know Mike gets a little excited because he's really protective of his friends, but you are what's kept me going these last two years. That last year of high school, when I realized that they all knew I was gay, I wanted to run, or hide, or something. I just wanted to get away from the looks and the whispering, but I knew that I had to finish if I wanted to see you again. Then, after everything happened with Mosely, I couldn't let myself give up. I hadn't heard from you, and a little voice inside me just kept telling me that you were in trouble. *My* Jamie would have done anything to keep in contact with me, and the fact that you hadn't… it scared me so badly." Brian's voice had fallen to a whisper, and the pain in it filled my chest with such longing that it ached.

"God, I wanted to. I kept looking for ways, but we had no access to the Internet, and they monitored all of our mail. I couldn't contact you because I thought that my mom would call the state on your parents, and no matter how much I needed you, I wouldn't risk that. You were safe with the Schreibers. I knew I just had to survive until we were both eighteen. But the more I thought about you, the more I hated myself because I was so selfish to hold you to that promise. I didn't think you'd be able to get to California, or that we could be together. I didn't have anything to offer you. So, I wrote you that letter, and I gave you up. It was the hardest thing I've ever done because I needed you so fucking much." The tears welled in my eyes as I remembered how my hands shook more with each word I wrote. I'd cried so hard that night as I waited for dawn and the food delivery truck to come.

"I knew, as soon as I read the letter. I knew that you were in trouble and that you needed me. I'd almost decided to take the scholarship and go off to college because I didn't even know if you were still in California. I packed that night and got on a bus the next day. You got me through that too. I never would have had the courage to leave Alabama and start a new life here without you." He squeezed me tighter in his arms, and I stared at the blanket covering my chest.

"I ruined your life," I admitted. The choking sadness in my voice must have caught him off guard because he turned me in his arms and grabbed my chin. He forced me to look up into his face.

"You *saved* my life. Things here in San Diego are so much better for me than they ever were in Alabama, except for our time together.

Do you remember what high school was like for me before you left? You were my only friend. People tolerated me when you were around, but when you weren't, they were fucking cruel. I have amazing friends here who care about me. I have a social life. I have a life, period. I know that you and my parents don't like me doing porn, but since I got over my initial embarrassment, I don't have a problem with it. Nick, Julio, and some of the other guys are teaching me the production side of things, and it's really interesting. I have fans, Jamie. You should see some of the comments that people make on the boards and on the social media sites. I finally feel attractive—sometimes I even feel kinda sexy." Brian laughed, and the light-hearted sound contrasted sharply with the earlier seriousness. I had to smile at him.

"You are sexy, Brian. God, I used to think of all kinds of horrible things after gym class just to stop myself from getting hard when I saw you. At night, I used to jack off thinking about you and dreaming about a time when we could be together like this." I swept my arm over us to indicate our position. "Just sitting in each other's arms, totally unafraid of being discovered. If I weren't so fucking scared about what Steven is going to do when he finds us, it would be a dream come true."

"I will not let him hurt you again," Brian murmured against my neck. "I'd give my life to protect you." The intensity of his voice underscored just how much he meant what he said. It felt different, though, than having that same conviction about him. The idea of him following through with that sentiment scared me to the core, where dying for him didn't.

"It won't come to that."

"No, it won't, because we've been very careful. He's not going to find you, and he's not going to hurt Alex," he told me softly, and I didn't argue because I didn't want to upset the sweet moment. Nestled in his arms, loved and happy, I knew it could be taken away at any second, so I clung to it as tightly as I could.

"So, what happens now?" I asked after a few minutes. The topic wasn't something that I wanted to talk about, not while I sat sheltered in the warmth of Brian's arms, but I needed to know the plan. My life had been out of my control for such a long time, and I didn't like that feeling. Brian yawned quietly and snuggled closer under the blanket. Our combined body heat took the chill out of my bones, which helped with the dull ache I felt all over.

"We'll stay here a few more days so that you can get a little stronger, and then Leo will take you and me to our new apartment. Nick is going to make sure that Alex and Mike shoot on the same schedule for a while in case O'Dell shows up at the studio. They're going to start locking the door from the first to the second floor just in case, and there are usually a bunch of other guys around so Alex won't be left alone for a while. Alex, Leo, and Emilio can drop by the apartment while I'm working so you won't be lonely. Once your stomach has healed, we can do whatever you want. We can stay in San Diego in the new apartment, or we can go back to Alabama. As long as we're together, Jamie, it doesn't matter to me where we are." Brian's voice trailed at the end, and I knew that it was a lie. Brian loved San Diego. He'd just admitted that it was the only place he'd ever felt like he belonged. I wouldn't take that away from him, not after what he'd risked for me. Besides that, I fucking hated Alabama. I didn't have anything there worth going back for.

"I think we should stay in San Diego if we can figure out how to stay safe." I kissed the side of his neck as if in punctuation of my statement. I felt his throat vibrate under my lips and asked, "What?"

"I said thank you," he whispered. My burn screamed in protest as I turned my body so that I could kiss him properly, but just as my lips touched his, one of the doors across the small room opened and Emilio came through with a grocery bag in one hand and his keys in the other.

"Hey, guys," he said with a wave of his keys as he went into the small kitchen. I lost track of him then, though I could hear him putting things in cabinets and some kind of glass bottles in the refrigerator. It took several minutes for him to come back into view and drop into the chair across from where we were on the couch. He flopped one perfectly sculptured, tanned leg over the side, slouching and comfortably spread. A pink flip-flop dangled from his foot as it bounced anxiously. His loose shorts gaped a bit in the leg, and I could see a flash of turquoise beneath. Em really was a beautiful guy and probably the only guy, besides Brian, I'd really enjoyed having a scene with at Hartley.

I found myself rubbing Brian's bare thigh absently under the blanket.

"How was the shoot?" Brian asked, but the underlying tension in his voice betrayed his nerves. The shoot wasn't what he wanted to know about. Em understood that and got right to the point.

"He sat in his truck from the time I got there until the time I left. I think he was waiting for someone else. You and I were never that openly friendly, Jamie. I doubt he even thought to stop me and ask me where you were. When I asked around at the studio, he hadn't bothered any of them. Either he's biding his time, or he's waiting for Mike, Alex, or Brian." Em met Brian's eye, and I saw a look of understanding pass between them. Brian understood that Steven wouldn't just give up.

"This is crazy. I don't want to put anyone—" I started, but before Brian could stop me from finishing the sentence, Em put a hand up.

"Jamie, we all knew what we were getting into. I got the shit kicked out of me practically my whole fucking life, and I'll be damned if I'll let it happen to someone else when there's something we can do about it." He looked around and then asked Brian, "Speaking of, where are Mike and Alex?" I snorted, and Em's eyebrow lifted.

"They're fucking their brains out upstairs," I said, and the sadness in Em's face startled me. Almost as if someone had flipped a switch, the light, bubbly attitude that I associated with him turned sullen.

"I'm going to go take a shower. Maybe we can order some food if you're up for it. Or, I guess I could always go out alone." He stood up in one quick, lithe movement and headed for the door that led to the third floor.

"Em!" Brian called just before he was through the doorway. Em turned, faked a smile, and told Brian he'd be back down in a little bit. He called Brian "baby boy," and I found that it didn't bother me nearly as much as when Mike called him "baby." The door closed, leaving us alone in the room again.

"I don't understand," I told Brian and made an effort to sit up a little more so that I could turn to look at him. His face looked tense, troubled, and I stroked his cheek with my fingers. The circles under his eyes bothered me. He looked tired, and much older than anyone who was about to turn nineteen should look.

"Are you sure you want to talk about this? You got pretty pissed in New Orleans," he warned. I looked down at the blanket again, and shame caused my face to flush hotly. When I'd heard a few weeks before that Mike, Emilio, and Brian used to have a sexual relationship together, I hadn't taken it well. I could see in his hesitation that Brian feared another overreaction. We sat in silence for a long time before he sighed and, without touching my skin, linked his fingers over my abdomen.

"Yeah, and I'm sorry about New Orleans. I should have talked to you about it, but I was shocked and upset. I didn't handle it well," I admitted, and my flaming face heated up again. "I'd just been so happy that week, being with you, and when I saw you with them and Em said that you guys...." I looked away. Even though I knew Mike was right, that I had no right to be angry with him, it still hurt.

"Em has been sad lately because Mike's been with Alex and I've been with you, and it's not the three of us anymore. I think he feels lonely and left out," he confided.

"Yeah, I don't blame him." My voice sounded bitter, and I didn't have the heart to try to soften it with a smile.

"I couldn't find you." Brian's voice was so quiet that I almost didn't hear him. "It hurt every day. One night, they took me out to a club to try to get me to loosen up, and I got drunk for the first time. When I woke up, I was... I was naked in bed with Mike. I felt so sick—not because of the hangover, but because I had betrayed you."

The rage filled me before I could think, and I tried to get up.

"He got you drunk and... and... raped you? Motherfucker!" The last word was a cry of pain when my burned stomach clenched as I finally made it to my feet. Adrenaline rushed through me as I heard Brian scramble off the couch after me, and I charged toward the stairs.

"Jamie, stop!"

I didn't. Injuries or no, I was going to take his fucking head off. Then I might feed him his own dick. The door opened in front of me, and Em almost ran into me as he shook out his damp hair. He was barefoot in just a pair of old, faded jeans, and I might have appreciated the sight more if I weren't so fucking angry.

"Whoa," Em said as I pushed him out of the way. Brian caught up with me and, rather than grabbing me around the waist, hooked his arms up under mine in a half sleeper hold.

"Fucking let me go!" My feet came off the ground as I kicked up, trying to break his hold. The pain I felt from my injuries was nothing compared to the rage. That bastard hurt my Brian, and I wanted to make him hurt. With single-minded determination, I grabbed at Brian's hands, desperate to throw him off me. I couldn't even explain how out of control I felt as the anger rippled off me in waves.

"What the fuck?" Em asked as he joined Brian in trying to restrain me, which just made me angrier.

"I'll tell you in a minute," Brian called over my frantic curses as I flailed. They worked together to pull me back toward the couch. I kicked out, knocking over one of the chairs.

"Who the hell is yelling down here?"

I looked up to see Mike coming through the door, looking a bit disheveled. Alex came through the door right behind him, and he was more than a little tousled. It looked like we had pulled them out of bed. *Good. Fucker!* I tried harder to get away from Brian and Em because I no longer had to climb the stairs to get at that bastard.

"Jamie, what's wrong?" Alex asked, and it pained me to realize through my fury that he sounded scared.

"Yeah, what the fuck is princess on about now?" Mike looked somewhat bored with the scene, but I noticed that he stepped slightly in front of Alex to protect him. Like I'd ever hurt Alex!

"You motherfucker! You got him drunk and raped him? Do you drug Alex, too? Is that how you get guys because you're such a fucking pansy?" I heard Brian mutter a low curse under his breath, and Em snorted.

"What the fuck are you talking about? So Brian and I fucked. Jesus, get over it!" Mike said sarcastically. "Besides, I don't have to rape anyone! They fucking line up at the door. If I'd raped him, would we have done it like rabbits for months after that night?"

"Not helping!" Brian yelled as I tried to get away from him again. He motioned for Mike to go back upstairs and finally succeeded in getting me down onto the couch. "Alex, get the oxy! Please, it's next to the bed upstairs!" Alex turned and ran up the stairs.

"Are you sure you guys are going to be okay with him?" Mike asked, his face showing real concern for the first time. My rage was out of control—I recognized that on some level—but Mike was the only person I wanted to direct it toward.

"He's better with me than he is with you, asswipe!" I yelled over Brian's shoulder, and I fought harder against the grip that Em and Brian had on me. All I wanted to do was beat his fucking face in.

"Brian, what's wrong with him?" Em asked softly as he held my legs against the couch. Brian's voice sounded pained and winded when he told Em that he didn't know.

"Mike, please, go upstairs or in the kitchen or something. You're just upsetting him more." Brian's voice cracked, and I watched the prick go back out the door that led to the third floor and slam it behind him. I still wanted to fuck him up, so I jerked my arms away from Brian, but he held firm. Alex returned then and handed the pills to Em.

"I'll get him some water," Alex said, and the fear still hadn't left his face.

"I've got it," Brian said, and in an instant had straddled me on the couch. Grabbing my face with both hands, he forced me to look him in the face and begged me to calm down. I didn't know how to calm the rage that seemed to have taken over my body. So I just focused on Brian's face, scared for the first time about losing control. When I stopped struggling, he wrapped his arms around my neck and just held me for several long minutes and then handed me two small pills and the can of soda from my tray. "Please, Jamie, take these." I started to shake my head, but he added, "For me, honey. It will make me feel so much better."

Unsure what he meant by that but desperate to make him happy, I let them help me sit up, popped the pills in my mouth, and took a long drink of the flat soda. Brian stayed in my lap, careful not to touch my stomach. He rested his head on my shoulder, stroked my hair, and tried to calm me. It helped. Between his touch and the slow infusion of pain medication into my blood, the rage started to leave me. I felt drained and rather sickened by my behavior, though residual anger still clung to my heart at the thought of Mike taking advantage of Brian.

"Did he hurt you?" I whispered into Brian's ear.

"Mike? No, of course not. He didn't… didn't rape me. I was so alone and hurt and scared. He just… he wanted to make me feel better. He didn't hurt me," he whispered back with a small kiss on my cheek. "I'm sorry that it hurts you. I'm sorry…. You've been through so much and…."

"Shh…." I stroked his face with my fingers and then pulled him closer to kiss him. His elbow touched my stomach, but I didn't move. I couldn't move, so I clenched my fists against the pain because I just wanted to feel him. "You thought that I'd given up on you, on us. I hate that it had to happen because we were apart, but I can't be angry with you for it. It happened after we broke up."

A strange look passed over Brian's face, but he didn't say anything.

"What?" I asked, almost reluctantly.

"I didn't know we *had* broken up. I just thought that circumstances got in the way, and now that… never mind. It's fucking stupid." He got up from my lap, and I missed the feeling of his body. I wanted to follow him when he went into the kitchen, but the oxy was making me feel sleepy, dizzy, and kind of slow. When I tried to get up, the room spun, and I fell back onto the couch.

"Hey, now," Em said, and it startled me because I had forgotten he was still in the room. He dropped down onto the couch beside me, pulling one leg up between us as he faced me. "He just went to put the tray away, babe. He'll be right back."

"Why do I keep screwing shit up with him? I can't even figure out why he would still want me." I put my head in my hands to stop the room from spinning. He either didn't hear me, or understood that I was rambling disconnected nonsense, because he didn't say anything about it.

"Come on, lie down. You can't be feeling too great after the morning you've had." Em grabbed a throw pillow from the other side of the couch before holding his arms out. Too tired and upset to argue with him, I fell over with my head on the pillow in Em's lap. He began to stroke my short hair.

"I seem to remember being in this position with you before…," he said, and I smiled at the amusement in his voice. I knew that he was referring to me blowing him in our scene together. It was eighth-grade humor, but it still lessened the weight that had settled in my chest. Brian came back in the room then and, rather than comment on our position, merely sat on the floor at Em's feet. I reached down and took his hand.

"I want for us to be together more than anything," I told him. "I just don't understand why you would want to be with me. I'm broken, Brian." He pulled my hand up to his lips and kissed it.

"You're not broken, baby. You're just a little banged up, a little bent. I want to be with you because I can't imagine not being with you. I can't imagine not loving you, and I don't want to. I want to come home to you every night and kiss you good morning every day." His voice was soft, but strong, and though I didn't think it was even possible, I felt myself falling more deeply in love with him.

"I want that too," I admitted. For the first time since my goddamned parents had dragged me kicking and screaming from his arms, I thought maybe there was hope for us. Even though the thought of Steven finding us scared me, even though I didn't have a job or any money, and even though Brian was still doing porn, I thought maybe, just maybe, we could find a way to make it work.

"Really?" Brian asked, his voice so full of hope that it hurt my heart.

"Brian, I know that I don't have anything to offer you right now. I have to get clean, find a job, and get back on my feet, but I can't deny either of us what we could have together. I love you so much, Brian. Can we try to make it work?"

"Oh, God," Brian cried, jumped to his knees, and wrapped his arms around me.

"Uh, guys? I would really appreciate it if you'd stop molesting me if you're not going to get me off," Em said and shifted slightly under me. Brian laughed and pulled his hands back, because while they were hugging me, they were also rubbing against Em's crotch.

"Sorry, babe," Brian said as he leaned forward and kissed Em lightly on the lips.

"Damn, I was really hoping you'd pick option number two," he told Brian, but his eyes were sparkling with laughter.

"Maybe when I'm feeling better," I told Em as they both gaped at me.

I just winked.

CHAPTER FOUR

"I'M GOING to pull the van around and back it up to the rear entrance. We can keep the doors partially closed so that no one sees him coming out the door or getting in the van. I'll make sure no one is following us. Mike and Alex, Julio and Tony, and Andy and Pete will be flanking us on the way to the apartment, so they can help keep an eye out," Leo said as he grabbed his keys from the desk.

"Are you sure all of that's really necessary?" Brian asked and looked at Mike, who shrugged.

"I don't want to take any chances with you guys. This guy is dangerous, and we don't want him to know where Jamie is, for all of our sakes," Leo said, forestalling any response Mike would have made.

"Okay, Brian, do you have everything you need? Medical supplies? Oxy? Food?" Leo asked.

Brian nodded. "Mike and Alex have the rest of my clothes and stuff in their trunk. Alex and I stocked the food yesterday while Mike was at work." Mike glared at Alex, but he shrugged.

"Brian's practically a black belt, babe, and we were surrounded by people. I know you're worried about me, but I can't live the rest of my life in hiding. Brian's going to teach me and Jamie some self-defense stuff once Jamie's feeling better. But… I love that you want to protect and take care of me," Alex said, punctuating it with a short, chaste kiss on Mike's lips. Mike pressed his forehead against Alex's and whispered something that I didn't hear, but that made Alex smile and kiss him again.

"So, we're ready," Brian confirmed to Leo and folded his arms in front of his chest as he stood next to where I sat on the common room couch. The members of our little mission stood in pairs around the room, which felt much less confining than Alex's small bedroom upstairs.

"Okay then, let's do it."

I held Alex's ridiculous pink kitty pillow over my stomach to protect it as I walked carefully down the stairs toward the back entrance. Every step felt like agony, but I refused to let it stop me. I had promised Brian that I would become the man he needed me to be. I would be strong for him, even if I couldn't do the same for myself. I stumbled about halfway down and caught the railing for balance. The motion pulled the top of my body in a different direction than the bottom and stretched my abdomen painfully. I sat down hard on the stairs in an effort to catch my breath.

I could hear someone racing down the stairs behind me while Brian stood next to me. It seemed that he couldn't quite decide what to do to help me. His hand hovered over my shoulder as if he were afraid to touch me. Helplessness radiated from his soft brown eyes, making me want nothing more than to reassure him, but I couldn't right then.

"Jamie, are you okay?" Alex asked, and I felt him sit on the stairs right behind me. His touch wasn't as hesitant, and he put a small hand on my cheek, like he was checking me for fever.

"Yeah, I just lost my step, was all," I replied and pulled myself up using the railing. Alex put his hands under my arms to steady me, and we made it down the last dozen stairs without further incident. Even through the oxy I'd taken just half an hour before, my stomach and back ached. Though the pain had lessened slightly since Brian took care of me last weekend, it was still intense if I moved too fast or lost my balance.

At the bottom of the stairs, Leo, Mike, and Brian stood to the side while Alex helped me into the van. The sunlight, mostly blocked by the obtrusive vehicle in the doorway, streamed in through the grimy windshield, allowing me to navigate the large cargo area. When Alex climbed out of the van, Brian took his place next to me, and I leaned against him. He wrapped an arm carefully around my shoulders and told Leo we were ready.

The doors closed with a loud bang that reverberated through the empty space. We heard muffled noises outside, and I assumed Leo was giving the other guys instructions. They had planned moving me from one safe house to another with such formality that it scared me. The seriousness with which they were taking my safety reminded me of just how much danger all of us were in. I'd relaxed a little being with Brian the last week, but it wouldn't take long for Steven to find the boarding house since a few of Nick's models lived there. He'd only need to follow any of them home one night, and they would be exposed.

It was crazy. I knew I should go back to him so he didn't hurt anyone else, but I just couldn't stand the thought of leaving Brian again. It was so selfish, even for me.

"Are you still in a lot of pain?" Brian asked, his voice soft and sad. I shook my head and then rested it on his shoulder. He pressed his cheek to my forehead in response, and we waited quietly while Leo climbed into the driver's seat and started the van with a rumble. The metal beneath us vibrated, and I put my hand on Brian's knee. We lurched a bit when Leo hit the gas and started us toward our new home.

The drive turned out to be longer than I expected.

"Where is the apartment?" I asked as I pulled my knees up almost to my chest and felt a twinge in my stomach when the skin stretched. We'd driven for almost forty-five minutes, and it felt like we were still on the highway. The rate of speed held constant with no stops and starts like you would normally find in city traffic. My ass was going to have permanent marks from the grooves on the metal floor.

"Oh, the apartment that Leo found for us is kind of far from the boarding house, but it's also far from the studio and from O'Dell's apartment. The neighborhood isn't great, but it's clean and safe."

At first, I felt anger at myself for forcing him to move from the nice neighborhood that contained the boarding house, but I stopped the thought. It had been his decision to move, his decision to take me in the first place. If we were going to make a relationship work between us, we had to not only accept each other's decisions, but also start making our decisions together. Based on our conversation from a few days before, we were a couple again. One thing I'd learned since I'd found Brian in that porn studio just a few months ago was that I didn't need to protect him. Back in Alabama, I'd always tried to keep him under my wing, both in school and outside of it. He'd always seemed so vulnerable to me, and I never wanted to let anything hurt him. But it seemed that in the last few years, our roles had reversed. I was the vulnerable one, and he continued to keep me under *his* wing.

God, I loved him for it.

"We're getting close," Brian said as he craned his neck to see out of the windshield. I hadn't bothered to look because I doubted I'd know where I was anyway. The only places I ever saw in San Diego once Steven took me in were his apartment, the studio, the grocery store, the library, and the occasional restaurant. I'd been in the city for two years, but I'd never really seen any of it. "It's just off the highway."

The van slowed, and we turned off onto another street. My excitement grew with every foot that brought us closer to the apartment. Just the idea of living with Brian, being able to see him every day and share my life with him, put the fear of Steven to the back of my mind for a while. I still felt pain, but the anticipation seemed to lessen the impact.

When we stopped and Leo turned off the ignition, I looked at Brian with the biggest smile I'd felt on my face in a long time. He smiled back and kissed me, taking his usual care to be gentle, but I didn't want to be gentle. Tossing the kitty pillow to the side, I straddled his lap and deepened the kiss, threading my fingers in his long curls. I loved the way he moaned against my mouth, the way his hands caressed my lower back as he kissed me.

The harsh light from the opening van door broke us apart, so I crawled off Brian's lap and out of the van before Leo could comment. Only when I stood on the street did I feel exposed and vulnerable. Looking around, I tried to spot Steven's truck, but the only vehicle I recognized was the black Jeep that Mike and Alex climbed out of. I spotted Julio and the other guy, Tony, coming up the sidewalk, but I didn't see Andy and Pete.

"Come on, babe. I can't wait to show you," Brian said, took my hand, and pulled me away from the van. The building we walked toward resembled an old roadside motel. Huge wooden railings wrapped around the two-story structure, which had doors spaced at regular intervals. To the right sat a dumpster partially surrounded by a high wooden fence covered in graffiti. A guy in oversized jeans and a dingy, once-white ribbed tank top watched us as he threw a couple of bags into the dumpster.

Brian led me past the dumpster and through an iron gate, which wasn't locked. Passing the stairs that led up to the second floor, he went to the third door, marked "107," and fished his keys from his pocket.

"Your copy is inside. I got two sets from the landlord," Brian said as the lock disengaged and the door swung open. He stood back and let me walk into the dark apartment first, moving to the side as we walked in to flip on the light switch next to the door. The first thing I noticed was the large sleigh bed on the far side of the room. A gaudy comforter peeked out from the foot of the bed, covered in large red, black, white, and gray concentric geometric shapes. As I moved into the small studio apartment, I looked to my left and saw Alex's couch and television stand, complete with his flat screen. So, while he had stored a lot of his stuff at the boarding house, he'd also lent some of it to us so we would have something to sit on. I promised myself, then and there, that when I got back on my feet, I'd do something very special for Alex.

Brian wrapped his arms around me from behind, careful not to touch my stomach, and whispered, "Welcome home, baby." I turned in his arms, anxious to share this amazing moment with him. It didn't matter that there were five other guys scattered through the small apartment. Brian and I were living together, which was what we'd wanted for so long. Something in my life finally fucking went right.

"Uh, we're going to just… yeah," Alex said with a laugh as he tried to herd Mike, Julio, Leo, and Tony from our living room. I opened my eyes to see the other guys setting down an array of boxes that contained Brian's clothes from the boarding house. When I just closed my eyes again and kissed Brian with everything I had, the guys gave a few wolf whistles and headed toward the door.

"You guys can stay for a while," Brian said halfheartedly as he broke our kiss, but he didn't let go of my waist. I nuzzled against his neck, waiting for them to leave. Of course I appreciated what they had done for us, but God, I wanted to be alone with Brian. Even if we did nothing more than just lay in bed kissing until we fell asleep in each other's arms, that would be a perfect night for me.

"Dude, if I wanted to see that, I'd buy the DVD," Tony said with good-humored sarcasm, and Brian snorted. The other four guys filed out after exacting promises from Brian that he would text them later. The only one to stay was Leo, who closed the door behind the others.

"I wish you would have stayed at the boarding house, where we could protect you," he told Brian, and I could hear the emotion in his voice. He shoved his hands into the pockets of his jeans and stood near the door. In the short time I'd known him, I don't think I'd ever seen Leo so shaken.

"Leo, I couldn't stay there with him. It put the other guys in danger. We'll be fine here, and we'll be careful, I promise."

"You better be, kid. You and Mike mean a hell of a lot to me. I couldn't stand it if anything happened to either of you." Leo pulled Brian into a one-armed hug, and I moved back out of the way so they could have their moment. I liked that Brian had so many people looking out for him. It didn't surprise me, though. I'd known all my life that Brian was special, and if people would look past his shyness and his status as a foster kid, they'd see what a beautiful soul he had. It thrilled me that he'd finally found that kind of acceptance here.

"I'll text you later," Brian promised, and double-locked the door behind Leo when he left. Finally alone in our new apartment, Brian was anxious to show me everything about it. We walked past Alex's couch and into the tiny kitchen, where he showed me how he'd organized it. Then he pulled me around the corner to show me a bathroom no bigger than our half bath back home. The room was just big enough to hold a tub with a shower, a sink, and a toilet. The barren white walls gleamed, as they did in every other room we'd seen. I didn't care. Brian and I were together, and we had a roof over our head. Everything else, we'd work out.

"Are you hungry?" Brian asked as he took a half step toward me. His gaze had almost turned predatory, and there was only one thing that I wanted right then.

"No." I moved another step closer to him.

"Want to watch a movie?" He smiled, and the expression just made butterflies erupt in my stomach.

"No."

Our lips met first as we stood next to our new, shared bed, and then his fingers ruffled the back of my short hair as our limbs wound around each other. I caressed his face with one of my hands, feeling the stubble from the day scratch against my palm. The way his body hummed under my hands, his hard chest rubbing against mine, made my heart pound, and I moaned into his mouth. His breaths were harsh against my face, as I'm sure mine were against his.

"We shouldn't do this. I don't want to hurt you," Brian murmured against my lips as I pulled at his shirt. Our mouths met again as I succeeded in tugging his T-shirt up over his nipples. Finally, he moved back just enough to allow me to get the shirt over his head. It hadn't even hit the ground before he was kissing me again. My trembling hands explored all the delicate lines of his bare back, and his fingers slid down my back into the waistband of my loose sweats.

"I want to touch you," I whispered as I pulled my own shirt over my head. "It doesn't have to be anything intense. Just lay down in bed with me, and let's see what happens. I promise we'll be careful." I wanted our first night in our own place to be about love and hope, not regret and pain. Against my cheek where his forehead rested, I felt a small nod. Pulling down my borrowed sweats, I took my new briefs with them and stood naked before him. Brian stepped back to look at me, and I saw his eyes cloud over with pain as he again took inventory of my injuries. His sadness made my heart clench.

Reaching out, I tilted his chin up so that his eyes met mine, and his expression softened. With a small kiss, I moved past him to drag back the covers and climb into our new bed. *Our bed.* The sheets had a stiffness to them that reminded me of a new shirt. My half-hard cock showed interest as Brian smiled down at me. He opened his fly and tugged his jeans and boxers down long, muscled legs. I tried not to think about how perfect his skin was while the burn and my other injuries had permanently scarred mine. I pushed away the thought that he would be better off finding someone whole, because he didn't want someone whole—he wanted me.

As he started to climb into bed with me, he stopped and jumped off again. I didn't understand for a minute until he strode to the front door and turned off the light.

"In case we fall asleep," he explained when he finally reclined on his side next to me on the bed. The light coming in from the window over our heads allowed me to see his beautiful face as he hovered above me. When I lifted up to kiss him, Brian put one arm behind my head while his other hand stroked my cheek. I let one hand fall back above my head, and our fingers intertwined as he explored my mouth with his. My other arm nestled under his body, and I ran my hand up and down his bare back. I reveled in the feeling of his skin, the scent of his body, and the safety of his arms.

With me on my back and him on his side, he half draped himself over me, being careful not to touch the bandage on my abdomen. I loved his weight against my chest, his fingers entwined in mine, and the way his deep, probing kisses made me throb. Everything about Brian turned me on. He let go of my hand and rubbed my chest, just lightly enough for an electric buzz to shoot down my spine. My nipples hardened when he stroked the small patch of hair between them and then lower. I rested my free hand on his arm to have a connection with him and stroked gently up to his shoulder.

"How are you feeling, baby? Are you hurting?" He whispered between tender kisses on my neck. I found it hard to focus with his hands and mouth working in tandem on my body.

"Please don't stop," I pleaded, surprised to hear how hoarse my voice sounded in the whisper. "This is the best I've felt in years. We're in *our* bed, Brian. *Our bed.* I love you so much, and I'm going to make myself worthy of your trust and your love. This is the beginning of something special, baby, I promise." His hand came back up to my face, and he cradled it as he kissed me, sealing our promise to each other.

His mouth left mine, moving down over my chest to my nipple, and I pressed my head back against his arm. Pulling his arm out from under me, he slid down in the bed and used both hands to hold himself up as he teased each nipple. I noticed the ceiling fan over the foot of the bed only when the cool breeze from it drifted over my wet skin, and I shivered with unencumbered need. My back arched as I pleaded with inarticulate moans for him to continue. When he moved down further, skipping over my bandage to focus on my hip, I threaded my fingers into his curls. I tried not to pull, I did, but Jesus he felt good. Brian nipped my hip with a soft bite when I moaned his name.

When he took me into his mouth, I couldn't think of anything except the way his warm tongue felt on the head of my cock. I had no pain, no fear, just Brian overloading my senses, and a cry rose from my lips. My free hand found his shoulder, and I held on to him to keep from losing myself to a swirling sea of emotion. When his fingers crept below my balls and stroked at my entrance, for a moment, I really wanted him to make love to me. But when I shifted, the stinging in my burn hinted at the pain the act would bring.

"Brian, turn around," I panted and tugged on his shoulder. My cock slid from his mouth, and he raised his head to look at me.

"What?"

"Turn your body around, so I can—" I started, but he was already in motion, having figured out my meaning. I slid down in the bed so that my head was in line with his hips. He moved forward a bit and let his feet rest on his pillow before I took his rigid dick in my hand. Guiding it gently to my mouth, my lips vibrated as I moaned, feeling him resume the blowjob he'd started on me.

Brian's slick fingers slid into my ass, and I knew our sweet encounter wouldn't last much longer. I wanted him to come with me, so I put my own fingers into my mouth next to his cock and got them wet. As I rubbed them around his tiny hole, he moaned again, and a shiver shot through my limbs. Carefully, my fingers slid into him, and I teased him from the inside, trying to find that one perfect spot.

He found mine first. I whimpered and drew him deep into my throat.

His hips began to move, fucking my mouth slowly as my fingers ran across that tiny bump. Rhythmic cries flowed from his full mouth, muffled by my cock. I couldn't think. I could barely breathe as I raced toward that elusive pinnacle and my balls tingled. Brian's taste, his smell, filled my senses and reminded me, more than anything else, that it was *Brian*. The emotions nearly drowned me, and I sucked harder, faster, because I wanted to make him feel good, like I did. My free hand lay on his hip, and I traced small concentric circles on his skin even as I worked his prostate and took him as deep as I could into my mouth.

Brian's muscles tensed under my touch, and my dick fell from his lips. I felt his harsh breath on my skin as he rested his head against my thigh. The smooth rhythm of his hips faltered into jerky, uncontrolled thrusts as he cried my name, and I tasted his hot, salty come on my tongue. Listening to him, feeling him come, turned me on like nothing else, and as I swallowed around him, I wanted to come too. That wicked tingle had started deep in my groin. I took my hand off his hip and reached down to stroke my own cock while I teased the rest of his waning orgasm from him.

He moaned softly and, without moving his head from my thigh, covered my hand as I jerked off with his voice in my head and his come in my mouth.

"Brian," I whispered in a half moan. My fingers slipped from him as I rolled onto my back, his hand sped up and drove my hand up and down my rigid cock. The burn on my abdomen stung like a bitch as my muscles tensed and pulsed under the damaged skin. I gritted my teeth, unable to stop the chain reaction in my stomach and groin when hot jets of semen exploded from me as my hips slammed up to meet our joined hands.

It was like heaven and hell as the pain melded with the pleasure and the intensity of the moment. I closed my eyes, savored that feeling, and seared it into my memory. My heart raced, but my breathing started to slow as he swung his body around again so that he lay on his side next to me, propped on one elbow and looking down at me with a beautiful smile.

"That was amazing," he murmured and reached up with a sticky, come-covered hand to stroke my cheek. I stretched as much as my body would allow with the pain and wrapped my hand around the back of his neck. Pulling him down to me, I kissed him slowly, almost lazily, and it felt like our start to a whole new life together.

"I'm going to grab a towel from the bathroom. Don't get out of bed," he warned and kissed me again before disappearing from my side for a moment. I heard the water running in the bathroom, and then he came back with a black hand towel. He'd gotten half of the towel wet with warm water and used it to clean the come from my skin. I had the feeling he enjoyed the task because it seemed to take much longer than it needed to.

After he tossed the towel back in the direction of the bathroom, he climbed in bed next to me and opened his arms. Without hesitation, I crawled into them and rested my head on his muscled chest. His arms closed around me, and in our new bed, in our new place, it was the first time in a long time that I felt like I was home.

Brian would always be my home.

CHAPTER FIVE

WHEN I woke, I felt disoriented, and my heart began to race. I could feel my pulse in my temples as my eyes tried to pierce the darkness of the room. The size of the bed reminded me of being at Steven's apartment, as did the open space beyond the foot of it. Brian mumbled in his sleep and tightened his arm around my chest, and I started to calm. Closing my eyes, I could hear the faint thud of heavy bass in the distance like a slow, steady heartbeat. A cramp tore through my back from lying in the same position for hours, and I slid carefully out of Brian's arms. He grunted, shifted his body into the newly vacant space, and slept on. I could never get tired of watching Brian sleep because his angelic face relaxed and he looked peaceful.

My bladder insisted that I move from the bedside, and my mouth tasted like battery acid mixed with pond scum, so I went into the bathroom. As I stood in front of the toilet blissfully emptying my protesting bladder, I saw a couple of brand new toothbrushes and other toiletries sitting on the back of the sink. The care with which Brian had gotten the apartment ready made my heart ache. I had given him such a hard time, initially because I didn't believe he'd thought things out, that he'd acted on impulse. His actions over the last few days since I woke up in the boarding house had proved me wrong over and over.

After cleaning up a bit and brushing my teeth, I walked out into the living room area, still naked, and tried to navigate to the kitchen by feeling my way around the furniture. I made it to the open doorway and ran my hand over the walls, trying to find the light switch. Since the kitchen appeared to be around the corner and down a bit from the bed, I hoped that the light wouldn't bother Brian. I hadn't eaten since that morning, and I wanted to see if I could scrounge something up.

As my fingers found a switch on the wall and moved it, a dim fluorescent bulb above the stove illuminated the tiny space. A refrigerator, stove, microwave, and even a dishwasher filled the room with surprising efficiency. The linoleum floor gleamed in the low light, obstructed only by a thin navy blue rug that lay in front of the sink. A matching blue dishtowel hung from the handles of one of the drawers. It felt so domestic, so homey, that I couldn't help but smile.

The refrigerator held a bounty of food, including eggs, milk, and a couple of different kinds of lunch meat and cheese. It looked haphazardly stocked, as if it had been done in a hurry. Packages of bologna and sliced cheese were thrown in next to a jar of mayonnaise and a sealed bottle of mustard. Bacon peeked out from behind the first row of food, and I considered making bacon and eggs. A bit of toast and butter would seal the deal.

Out of curiosity, I opened the freezer to see what it contained. All thoughts of bacon and eggs were lost as I found the stash of frozen pizzas stacked one on top of the other, filling half of the freezer's space. Steven hated frozen pizzas, so I never even considered buying them when I lived with him, but I used to live on them back home in Alabama. When Mama would have her church meetings and Daddy worked, I'd pop a pizza in and hang out in front of our big screen in the living room, able to watch whatever I wanted. Mama never let me watch some of the shows that the other guys at school talked about because of the sex or what she considered "immoral" behavior. But when I was there alone, eating my frozen pizza and chips, I felt just like every other teenager on the planet.

Flipping through the different options, I picked a sausage and pepperoni and laid it on the counter. It took me a few minutes to figure out how to work the oven because the configuration of knobs and buttons was different from the oven I'd been using at Steven's apartment, but eventually it started to heat up. I sliced open the plastic wrapping around the pizza and left it sitting on the cardboard. After searching for a few minutes, I found a box of aluminum foil and a pizza cutter. It seemed fortune had smiled on me at last. It was strange to get so nostalgic, so excited, over fucking frozen pizza, but for those few minutes, I could be happy.

The oven reached the temperature I'd set, so I put the foil-lined pizza onto the top rack and closed the door. The small bistro table, just outside of the kitchen, had comfortable chairs. I looked back into the kitchen at the digital clock and calculated the eighteen minutes until my pizza would be ready. It was strange to be sitting at the table nude, but I felt comfortable here, and I didn't want to bother Brian by looking for my sweats.

After about twelve minutes, the smell of pizza started to waft through the apartment. I cringed back into my chair as I remembered the last time I'd baked tomato sauce and cheese. I remembered his face changing as rage consumed him. I remembered watching the plate fly toward me. I remembered wishing I'd left my sauce-splattered shirt on as the scalding cheese burned layers of skin off my stomach. The tears started before I could really understand why.

For the first time since it happened, I put my head down on the table and cried.

"Honey, what is it?" A hand stroked the back of my head and then rested on my neck. I sat up and wiped my eyes before leaning over and resting my head against Brian's naked hip. The anger and pain that I had felt just a moment before dissipated under his touch.

"It's something stupid. It's nothing," I mumbled and closed my eyes, letting his body warm me. He smelled like sleep, sweat, and a little like sex. It was intoxicating.

"It's not stupid if it upset you, baby," he answered and rubbed lightly between my shoulder blades. "Is that frozen pizza I smell?"

"Yeah, it's just about ready. Are you hungry?" I asked as I opened my eyes again and looked up at him. I loved his sleepy smile and the way his hair went everywhere. Small red lines, left by creases in the pillow, crossed over his pale cheek.

"Hell yes, I'm hungry," he said and leaned down to kiss my neck. In a low, sexy voice, he murmured, "And I'd like some food, too." He winked lewdly at me, and I laughed. God, it felt so good to be with him. I was so accustomed to being scared all the time, to watching every move I made so that I didn't get a fist to the jaw. With Brian, I never had to worry about that—ever.

"Want me to put another one in?" I asked, and scrambled out of the chair.

"I'll get it. I think I'll eat a whole pizza myself. I'm fucking starving." He put a hand on my shoulder and walked past me into the kitchen, so I sat back down, disappointed. After everything he'd done for me lately, I could at least make him a damn frozen pizza, but he didn't seem to think anything of it. He grabbed another pizza from the freezer, unwrapped it, and put it in the oven.

"Babe, I think the first one is ready. I'm going to take it out," he called, and I smirked as I stood. Walking into the kitchen, I waited for him to set the hot pizza on the counter and bend to close the oven door. I pressed my groin against his ass and put my hands on his hips. He stood slowly and half turned with a smile. The decadent feel of his bare skin against mine and the sweet smell of his skin made me want to skip the pizza and take him back to bed. When Alex helped to get the apartment ready, he bought us coconut body wash because it was something he liked. At first, I didn't care one way or the other, but after smelling it on Brian for the last couple of weeks, the scent made me hard.

"As much as I love to watch you take it out… you're naked, darlin'—it's already out," I told him in a low voice against his neck. He moaned, a deep animalistic sound in his throat. Reaching up and cupping the back of my head with his hand, he turned his head and captured my lips with his in a hot, slow, decadent kiss.

"You're making me hard," he whispered. I chuckled in his ear and ran my hand up his naked thigh before grabbing the pizza cutter just in front of him on the counter.

"Excuse me," I said, stepping around him to cut the first pizza, and heard a disappointed whine from behind me. I laughed, feeling more free than I had my entire life. Never before had I been able to tease and love Brian without fear. In Alabama, we were scared of being discovered. When I was with Steven, I was afraid of one of us getting hurt. But in the apartment we shared, I could love him the way that I wanted. Even though we stood naked and kissing in the kitchen, hunger won out at that moment over sex. We could always have sex afterward.

We could do whatever we wanted.

"Tease," he muttered. I heard the refrigerator open, and then he asked, "You want soda or beer?" Since I hadn't had one in a while, I would need to take another oxy soon, so I opted for the soda. He grabbed two sodas, a bag of chips, and a couple of paper plates before heading over to the table. I cut the pizza into four big pieces and used the aluminum foil to carry it to the table. Sitting across from each other, we shared our first meal together at our very own table.

THE next several days followed the same pattern as the first. Brian had taken a couple of weeks off from shooting and seemed to want to focus all of his attention on me and on our relationship. We talked for hours as we lay in bed or cuddled on the couch—about the time we spent apart, and about where we wanted to go from there. I agreed, reluctantly, that Brian should stay in porn for the near future. In order to afford the rent on the apartment without the income that he got from adult videos, we would both have to get decent jobs. In my case, that was unlikely since I hadn't even finished high school.

He wanted me to get my GED, which I absolutely agreed with. He also wanted me to take a few college courses, which I couldn't agree with. I needed to make some cash so that I could start contributing. It wasn't fair for Brian to pay all of our expenses. I wanted to work, and while I couldn't do porn anymore because my body was a roadmap of scars, there were things that I could do besides strip for the camera. On top of all of that, my addiction loomed on the horizon. The oxy kept my addiction tolerable, but soon, I would run out, and then I'd have a serious problem. I was determined to beat it. I would make Brian proud of me.

"Hey, you want to watch a movie tonight? We can stream it through Alex's DVD player and maybe order out for a little Chinese food," he suggested as he stood up from the couch where we had been talking. He stretched and yawned, and suddenly I felt guilty for keeping him cooped up with me for weeks. Between the days we spent in the boarding house and the time we'd spent in the apartment, he hadn't seen daylight in a while.

"I wish we could go out. God, it's like being in Alabama all over again," I complained. Pulling my feet up onto the couch, I wrapped my arms around my knees. "It's not fair that you're trapped in the apartment with me all the time. You should be able to go out and see your friends." I rested my chin on my knee. Since the burn had scabbed over and started to heal, I felt better.

"Well, they did ask me if I wanted to go to a club this weekend for my birthday since we couldn't go last weekend. Maybe we could talk them into dinner outside the city instead?"

"What day is it?" I asked as I felt the blood drain from my face. Brian's face fell, and he looked reluctant.

"It's the eighteenth." He tried to make his voice soft and soothing, but that didn't help soften the pain in my chest. After everything he'd done for me, I'd missed Brian's birthday. I didn't buy him a gift; I didn't make him dinner; I didn't even wish him a happy fucking birthday.

"Why didn't you say anything on Monday?" Horrified, I tried to think back to that day. He had gotten quite a few phone calls, but I figured the guys were just checking up on him. I'd been so completely self-absorbed that I'd missed celebrating a day for which I was truly thankful.

"I don't know—it's not a big deal. Besides, I know you. You would have wanted to get me something, and I didn't want you to feel frustrated that you couldn't." Without waiting for me to answer, he grabbed his cell phone, dropped back onto the couch, and dialed.

"Hey, it's me. Can we do dinner, maybe some place out of the city? I bet Alex wants to get out of the house too. Yeah, I don't care.

You guys pick something—I don't know where anything is. Thanks, man. Yeah, Saturday sounds good." He paused then, clearly listening as he glanced at me. "He's doing better. The burn's healing, and his *spirit is improving*," he said in a significant tone with a raised eyebrow. The fight kind of went out of me then because I knew he was right. Things had been going so well since we'd recommitted to each other. They'd been perfect, actually. Brian finished up his conversation, disconnected, and set his phone back on the side table.

"I'm sorry," I told him when he turned back to me. His eyes softened, and then he reached out and stroked my cheek. "There are so many more important things in our lives than a forgotten birthday. I just… it's important to me." Soft, yielding lips captured mine in a sweet kiss that quieted my apology. Without breaking the kiss, I crawled into his lap by straddling his legs.

"I forgot your birthday the year after you left," he whispered against my lips. My forehead pressed against his, and I felt him shake his head a fraction. "I remember feeling like something inside of me had broken. You were gone, and I hadn't even honored you enough to remember your birthday."

"We'll have a lifetime of birthdays to celebrate together," I murmured against his neck as I kissed it.

"I know how we can celebrate," I whispered against his ear and was rewarded with his shiver. We still hadn't made love because of my injuries, but I felt stronger every day. I thought maybe we could after our date on Saturday night for dinner with the guys. If I just mixed a little booze with the oxy, I wouldn't feel any pain. When I took my pills that morning, I noticed that there were only enough to get me through Saturday. We'd have to talk to Leo about getting more. Even though I'd tried to cut down on the number that I took each day so that I could make them last, they couldn't last forever.

To be honest, I was scared about what would happen when those pills ran out. I'd been taking them for two weeks. I may have become addicted to them. I didn't know if my body would still crave the coke or the ecstasy as well, but—like Leo told me the other day—I would have to take each day as it came.

I TORTURED myself for the next three days with images of making love to Brian, of Brian making love to me, and a number of other wickedly hot scenarios. We teased each other at every opportunity, sometimes making it to the bed before we sucked each other off, sometimes not. I found that the rug on the floor in front of the couch was surprisingly comfortable when I knelt on it to suck Brian as he reclined against the back of the sofa.

My hair had grown out since Steven's brutal cutting, and it even started to curl again at the ends. It made a great place for Brian to bury his fingers or pull when he came. God, I loved it when he tugged on my hair as he lost control. Once, when he filled my mouth and his fingers tightened in my hair, I lost control and came on the floor. My deep, resonating moans around his cock in my mouth kept him hard, and I got to watch him use that rainbow dildo I'd seen in New Orleans. I now understood why guys liked to see that in porn. Watching Brian writhe on the couch as he stroked his dick and fucked his ass made me come again as I stood over him.

Friday night, Mike and Alex went out and bought me something decent to wear since all of my clothes were still at Steven's apartment. Alex had great taste. I loved the form-fitting jeans and tight blue T-shirt I wore for Brian's birthday dinner on Saturday. For the last two years, I'd hated wearing clothes that were even the least bit tight because I felt exposed. It wasn't usually an issue since I'd been steadily losing weight for months. Even if Steven bought me something skimpy and tight, it hung off me within a few weeks. But, the way Brian's eyes lit up when he saw me made me feel sexy and special. With him watching me, I didn't seem to mind so much.

We held hands as we walked out through the iron gate toward Mike's Jeep sitting by the curb a few spots up the street. I felt anxious as my eyes scanned both sides of the street for the black truck that I knew would eventually catch up with me. I didn't see it, and I tried to hide my relief as I squeezed Brian's hand before letting go. I climbed up behind Mike while Brian sat behind Alex. Once I had the seatbelt fastened, I reached over and held his hand, and he kissed me with a loud smack.

I laughed, and my heart felt so light and free, I thought maybe it would burst from my chest. The bitterness about how my life should have been with Brian, the dark feelings I'd dwelled on for so long, began to burn off in the intensity of his love.

The four of us talked all the way to Point Loma, where Alex said we'd find the "best restaurant ever." It didn't matter to me what kind of place it was because it took nearly an hour to get there, and we could feel relatively safe. With a little luck, we wouldn't run into Steven or anyone that worked for him.

"Babe, did Nick ask you to dance at Big Boys tomorrow night?" Mike asked as he shifted the Jeep into the highest gear and reached for Alex's hand. Their fingers entwined as their hands rested on Alex's thigh. Begrudgingly, I found it sweet that Mike reached for Alex each time his hand was free. After the screaming match in the common room the night I found out how their sexual relationship began, Mike and I had come to a kind of impasse. He didn't fuck with me, and I ignored him.

"Yeah, but he said I didn't have to go," Alex replied. Scooting down lower in the seat, he pulled his knees up to rest against the dash.

"I really don't want you to go," Mike told him tenderly as he stole a glance at Alex's face. Alex lifted their joined hands and kissed the back of Mike's knuckles.

"I hadn't planned on going." Alex's smile as he looked over at his lover brimmed with happiness. It wasn't just a smirk, or a grin, but a truly happy smile. For a few minutes, I felt happy with them and forgot how Steven hunted me.

The anxious feeling returned to my stomach when we walked into the restaurant to find Emilio, Brandon, Brandon's wife Leslie, Josh, and Leo waiting for us. Steven wouldn't dare make a scene in a public place surrounded by so many people who knew who he was and where the police could find him. But again, Steven had never been particularly rational.

The huge, open-architecture restaurant featured clean lines and vaulted ceilings. Soft earth tones made up the color scheme, accented by plants throughout the room to give it a natural feel. One side of the room had a huge counter surrounded by people, but the rest encompassed a seating area with booths and tables full of smiling friends and even a few families. It reminded me of a high-end yuppie cafeteria.

Eight of us milled around, taking in the restaurant and waiting for a host to seat us until Alex quietly explained that the restaurant offered a more relaxed and casual atmosphere. He led us to a counter filled with food in the back, manned by smiling employees in muted T-shirts bearing the name of the place. Above their heads, a huge flat panel television showed us our options for dinner. Some of the stuff on the list I'd never even heard of, but Alex appeared totally in his element. Brian looked intrigued by the offerings, but Mike, Brandon, and Josh had similar expressions of confusion and disappointment.

"What the fuck is 'tabbouleh'?" Mike whispered to Alex, who rolled his eyes and giggled.

"Babe, you need to stop eating all your meals out of Styrofoam containers. Tabbouleh is a Middle Eastern salad with tomatoes and herbs." Alex reached down to entwine their fingers, and the tension left Mike's shoulders. The others must have been used to seeing Alex and Mike together at the studio, because no one gave them a second glance. Mike nodded, acknowledging Alex's advice, and he beamed back at Mike.

"Alex, what's 'quinoa'?" Brian tried to ask Alex, whose gaze hadn't left Mike's face.

"It's like rice, babe," I told him, and his brow furrowed—no doubt he was wondering how I knew that when he didn't. "Steven taught me how to cook." When the group fell silent, I couldn't believe I'd thrown Steven's name out so casually. Brian stared at me, but I just blushed. "I'm sorry, I didn't think before I said it. I only knew what quinoa was because it's one of the things he likes. He liked to eat healthy, which confused the hell out of me since he poisoned his body with drugs." Conversation started up again slowly, and Brian leaned in closer.

"Well, if it means no drugs, we can live on pizza for all I care," Brian whispered, and kissed my cheek. Of course, we both knew that was still a long road ahead, but we'd just deal with it as we'd been dealing with everything else.

"Kid, this is probably the gayest thing I've seen you do yet, and I've fucked your ass," Brandon said quietly to Alex with a laugh. Brian and I both looked around to see if his comment had been overheard. There were a few families with kids scattered around the restaurant. At first, Alex looked down at the floor in embarrassment, but Mike nudged him and winked. It looked like Alex's hand slid over onto Mike's leg as he steeled himself to respond. His face flushed slightly as he spoke.

"Well, Brandon, I see my fashion sense hasn't rubbed off. Does Mr. Rogers know you stole his sweater?" Alex asked haughtily, and

Mike snorted loudly. Brandon looked down at his tan-colored v-neck sweater. A white T-shirt peeked out from the bottom of the V. When coupled with the tailored jeans and shoes he wore, he did look much nicer than usual, but still not in the same league as Alex. Brandon glanced back up at Alex and smirked.

"It's about fucking time, kid. And actually, my wife made me wear this sweater because she thinks it makes me look respectable." Brandon snorted and lifted Leslie's hand to kiss it sweetly. "Imagine, a respectable porn star." We erupted in chuckles just as a woman asked Alex what he wanted from the food station. When we got to the end of the line, Brian grabbed a beer for me and got a soda for himself. He said we'd probably end up at a club afterward, and if he wanted something, he could drink there. I looked forward to the long pull from the bottle that would help to alleviate the tension in my back and shoulders.

After paying the cashier over Brian's protests, I followed Alex as he searched for a table large enough to accommodate eight of us. Finally, Brandon and Mike pulled together two good-sized tables in the back corner and grabbed an additional chair from an empty table nearby. Once everyone sat down, Mike lifted his beer.

"Happy birthday, baby—I hope your wildest dream comes true today," Mike said, and tipped the bottle forward. Brian blushed and glanced quickly at me. The other guys tipped their glasses to Brian, but I leaned over and kissed him instead.

"I know it's a few days late, but happy birthday, honey," I whispered, and I felt him smile against my lips.

"I kind of like this place," Mike said as he bit into the steak from his salad. "It's friendly and not pompous like some of the other restaurants downtown. I don't feel like I'm eating with the wrong fork here."

"Well, I love this place, so I'll let you bring me here whenever you want," Alex said with a grin, but then sobered quickly when Mike asked him how he knew about it. "My family lives a few blocks from here," he said quietly and put his fork down on the napkin next to his plate to take a long drink of wine. Mike put his hand over Alex's on the table but didn't comment.

"So, you guys want to go out after this? Alex, are there any good clubs around here?" Brandon asked, and Alex looked startled to hear him use his name. Usually Brandon called him "kid" or "boy" or worse. It seemed that all Alex needed to get Brandon off his ass was a little confidence. I was really glad he found that with Mike, even if the guy was an ass. So long as he wasn't an ass to Alex, things would be fine.

"I know where some good gay clubs are around here," Alex told him with a smirk, but Brandon just shrugged.

"Dude, I spend half my life fucking you guys. I don't care if it's a gay club so long as they have decent music and good beer. Besides, maybe my little girl and I can pick up a stray pup to fuck later." Brandon looked at Leslie, who had been quiet throughout dinner. Her eyes lit up as she slid one of her hands under the table, presumably to rest in Brandon's lap.

"I think that's a fantastic idea," she said, and then leaned over to whisper something in Brandon's ear.

"Oh yeah, I definitely think that's on the menu for later," he told her with a smile and then kissed her. For a second, I wondered what kind of relationship they must have if they picked up random people for sex. It reminded me about Brandon hooking up with the waitress in New Orleans.

Of course, it was none of my business, but I believed in monogamy. It bothered me that Brian had to fuck other guys to pay the rent. I knew from experience that they didn't necessarily have an emotional connection—it was just sex. That didn't stop it from needling at me when I waited for him at home while he fucked at the studio.

The banter between Brandon and Alex continued through the rest of dinner. Even Em and Brian got into it and gave Mike shit about how whipped he'd become with Alex. That started an entirely different discussion about whipping and bondage that I didn't need to hear when it came to Mike and Alex. Em practically bounced in his seat, ready to get to the club and dance. I thought he looked forward more to picking up a trick. Leo, who had been rather quiet during dinner as well, surprised us by mentioning that he wanted to go to the club.

As Mike's Jeep wove through the winding streets, Brian said he thought maybe Leo was lonely. He spent most of his time working on causes, maintaining the boarding house, or helping its inhabitants.

"I've been here a year, and I've never heard of him even going on a date," Brian confided as we pulled into the parking lot of an understated dance club.

"I've been with him a hell of a lot longer than that, and I've never seen him date," Mike amended with a sigh. "I don't know why. Leo is a hell of a guy. He deserves to find someone."

"Would you have said that six months ago, before you found Alex?" Brian asked with a smirk, and Mike turned to Alex.

"I see your point, but now that I'm happy, I want everyone to be happy." Mike slid his hand into Alex's and started walking toward the spot where Brandon had parked so that we could all go in together. Leo got out of Brandon's SUV and looked around slowly. It took me a minute to realize that he was scanning for Steven. I'd been so relaxed and happy since the restaurant, I had nearly forgotten about the danger. Chastising myself for the lapse, I followed the group to the entrance.

They shunted Brian and me into the middle of the throng, and I slipped past the guy carding without incident. It amazed me how these guys had perfected sneaking underage friends in with them.

I'd been to a few clubs with Steven, usually because he knew or could pay off the guy at the door. Of course, I never really got why anyone would want to go because dancing with Steven as he groped me on the floor always felt like dancing on stage in front of a drunken crowd. The hands, the pinches, and everything that I hated about the experience remained the same. The one and only difference between that and dancing on stage was that I could get drunk and not worry as much about being embarrassed.

I should have known that the experience with Brian would be completely different.

Brandon and Josh went up to the bar to get drinks while the rest of us found a table off to the side of the dance floor. Leo and Emilio scanned the crowd a few times, possibly looking for potential dance partners or even hookups. As I slid into the booth next to Brian, his arm went around my shoulders, and I relaxed into him. His lips pressed against the back of my neck, and I loved how perfect the night had gone so far.

"Are you going to dance with me tonight?" Brian murmured against my skin, and I could focus on nothing but the tingling feeling of his lips.

"It's your birthday celebration—I'll do whatever you want," I told him, and hoped that my expression looked halfway sexy. Without a word, he leaned over and pulled my earlobe between his teeth. I shivered at his warm breath in my ear.

"What if I said I wanted you to ride me until you came like a fucking geyser all over me?" The temperature in the room spiked suddenly. I reached back and threaded my fingers in his hair.

"I'd tell you that I'm not feeling well at all, and I think we should go home… right now," I whispered back, and slid my hand into his lap. He glanced around quickly and then grabbed my hand and slid it up to his crotch so I could feel the erection under his jeans. "Is that for me?"

"Uh huh," he moaned against my ear, and just as he started to rub my chest with light fingers, the guys came back with drinks. I pulled the baggie with the oxy out of my pocket and took one with the rum and Coke.

"Babe, you shouldn't be drinking and taking that stuff," Brian said quietly, and tilted my chin so that I looked at him as I sat sideways in the booth with my back against his chest. "Please be careful with that. I couldn't stand it if something happened to you."

"I'll switch to soda after this one," I promised. "I just want to have fun with you tonight without having to worry about shit, you know?" He nodded, wrapped his arms around my chest, and held me tightly against him while I finished the drink. Mike and Alex sat in a similar position across from us with Alex pressed back against Mike's chest. We tried to talk to them over the music, but mostly we just talked to each other, until Brian squealed behind me and smacked Mike's arm across the table.

"Ow, what?" he asked, caught off-guard by the sudden slap. Brian pointed not so subtly to the dance floor, and we all looked over to see Leo dirty dancing with a kid that couldn't have been older than I was.

"Well, I'll be damned," Mike said with a laugh. We decided to stay at the table for a while longer—until Leo had disappeared with his friend, actually—before we made our way out onto the floor. I hadn't really kept up with current music while I lived on the street or with Steven, but I felt really good and just let my body move with little conscious thought. Leo emerged after three or four songs and danced with us for a while. Brandon and Leslie found a sweet little twink who seemed to be just as into Leslie's groping as Brandon's hot looks. Mike and Alex danced almost illegally in our circle, surrounded by envious onlookers. A few guys tried to hook up with the couple for the night, but they were only interested in each other. It didn't take long for most of our group to decide that sex sounded better than dancing, and we called it an early night. Leo and Em wanted to stay, so Mike left his keys with Leo, and the rest of us piled into Brandon's SUV. It should have been able to sit seven adults, but we crammed in eight instead, including Brandon and Leslie's little twink, and Mike took full advantage of Alex ending up on his lap.

"Damn, I do want to sit on your dick, but please don't make me come in the car," Alex murmured into Mike's ear. It was nearly inaudible, but since I sat right next to them in the very back row of seats, I heard it clearly. I wished for time to go faster.

Even with the cramped seating arrangement in the car, I still felt great when we pulled up in front of our apartment complex. Mike put Alex in the seat he vacated and told him to stay there while he and Brandon got out. The SUV clock showed that it was nearly midnight, and the street beyond our windows was pitch black. Brandon and Mike looked around for a few minutes but didn't see any sign of Steven. Mike opened Brian's door to let us out, and then they walked us up to the apartment. I may not have felt very safe because, really, Brandon and Mike were no match for a gun, but it was nice of them to take such good care of us. In Mike's case, he wanted to protect Brian, but Brandon and I had always gotten along well.

"Make sure you double-lock the door," Mike told Brian once we were inside. He hugged Brian and kissed the top of his head before leaving again with Brandon. Brian turned the locks and watched through the window as Mike got back into the SUV. Once the silver vehicle had rounded the corner, Brian turned to me and wrapped his arms around me.

"Are you tired, babe?" he asked, and I loved the soft, sensual tone in his voice. Brian could be so fucking sexy without even trying.

"I believe you promised to let me ride you until I came all over you," I whispered and ran my tongue lightly around the shell of his ear. His shiver made me hard for him even before I felt his hands tighten on my waist to steady himself.

"I want to ride you instead. Is that okay?" he asked, and whimpered softly when I grabbed his ass in both hands and squeezed.

"Let's go to bed," I told him as I led him to the bed in the back of the room. He turned off lights on our way, and we undressed side by side under the moonlight filtering in through the window above our heads.

"I'm going to go clean up. I'll be right back," Brian said in a whispered kiss against the back of my neck. Turning, I kissed him back and then watched him walk naked into the bathroom nearby. The sound of running water came through the closed door, and I rummaged around for a few minutes in our side table. Condoms and lube were sitting in the drawer next to a few pillar candles. Knowing Brian, he had put the candles there in case of a power outage, but I liked the idea of making love to him by candlelight, so I pulled them out. I put two on his side table, one on mine, and then lit them with the matches that I also found in the drawer.

The water shut off in the bathroom, so I went to the door and knocked softly.

"Can I come in and brush my teeth?" I asked quietly, and the door opened. Brian put the small travel bag in his hand under the sink and closed the cabinet door. He grabbed both of our brushes from the medicine cabinet over the sink and handed mine to me. We stood side by side in front of the mirror and brushed our teeth in the nude. Anticipation pulsed through me as Brian's reflected eyes met mine and he smiled.

We left the brushes and toothpaste on the sink and turned toward the door. Brian stopped me with a hand on my arm, and I turned to look at him.

"You have toothpaste…," he said, and used his thumb to brush along my bottom lip. Covering his hand with my own, I held it against my face.

"Brian," I whispered and kissed the bed of his thumb. A low, desperate moan escaped him as his lips replaced his thumb on my mouth. Slowly, we moved out of the bathroom toward the bed. For every step he took backward, I took one forward to keep our lips together. I never wanted space between us again.

After several minutes, we reached the bed, and I watched as he climbed onto the big mattress and reclined back against the pillows. Crooking one finger at me, he invited me to join him in our bed. It was an invitation that I would never refuse.

I didn't kiss him but instead rolled him onto his stomach with his hips raised on my pillow. He looked back over his shoulder at me, trying to figure out what I would do. Rather than looking nervous, he appeared merely curious. Beautiful in the filtered moonlight, he relaxed on his stomach as the flicker of candles danced against his perfect skin. Starting at the soles of his feet, I rubbed every inch of his tender flesh. By the time I reached the tops of his thighs, he trembled under my hands.

Brian moaned deeply into the pillow when I massaged his back and shoulders. The sound made my cock pulse and leak drops of pre-come onto his ass as I straddled his hips. When the tension in his muscles had eased, I changed tactics. I'd intended to relax him with the massage, but I also wanted to excite him. Swiping the curls off the back of his neck, I pressed my lips there as the rest of my body pinned him against the mattress.

"Jamie," he moaned in a breathless whisper as he turned his head, but I wasn't done—not even close. The pain in my body couldn't quite make it past the fog of drugs and booze, and I felt good for the first time in weeks. I wanted to make my Brian feel good too. In fact, I wanted to give him a night of blissed-out sex that he could remember when he had to close his eyes and fuck other guys at work.

As soon as that image entered my mind, I shoved it away. I refused to think about that right then. In that moment, the only people who mattered were Brian and me.

I trailed long, tender kisses down his spine and felt him shift. It seemed that my sweet Brian was getting hard against the pillow beneath his hips. When I reached the dip in his back at the base of his spine, I nuzzled my face against it while he gasped. My name came again, with no real volume, as I watched his fingers tighten in the sheets. I cherished each of his quiet little whimpers when my lips ghosted over the perfect globes of his ass. He tensed as I teased between them, first with warm breath and then the very tip of my tongue.

I used my palms to hold him open so I could lick his tight little hole. He writhed under my mouth, and I grazed his rigid cock with the back of my hand as I wrapped my arms around his thighs to hold him still. I loved how spread open and vulnerable he was, just for me. Pumping his hips, he tried to touch my hand again, and I drove my tongue deeper into his ass.

"Oh my God," Brian squeaked into the pillow, barely loud enough for me to hear. It seemed to go on forever like that—his hips rolling under my touch, his sweet desperate sounds, and the taste of him on my tongue. Unable to stand it any longer, he reached between his body and the bed to stroke his dick. My own cock ached from watching the way he couldn't keep his hips still or his whimpers quiet.

"It's your birthday, angel… tell me what you want," I told him, and his face turned toward the sound of my voice without opening his eyes.

"Please, lay down. I want to sit on your cock." The hoarse request sounded like music. When I didn't move immediately, his beautiful eyes opened, and he looked back at me. Grinning at him, I got up on my knees and moved up to the head of the bed to lie next to him. As he blew out a long breath, he came up on his knees and moaned.

"My body feels like jelly," Brian whispered before crawling to the side of the bed. He picked up the condom and lube I'd set out earlier and fell back on the bed next to me. It took no time at all for him to roll the condom on my erection and coat it with lube. It felt like heaven to have his hand on me.

When he straddled my hips, I reached for him. Brian leaned forward and captured my lips with his in a soft, lingering kiss. Wrapping my arms around his back, I held him there in that kiss for several minutes. Every bit of the love and affection that we felt for each other exploded between us as he sank down onto me without breaking our kiss. He stole my breath away with his sharp inhale when my cock entered his body. The tight, hot feeling just beyond the barrier of the condom made me want to come as his ass came to rest against my groin. He tightened around me, and the need to come grew stronger. Grabbing his hips and holding them in place, I gritted my teeth and took several deep breaths. We had waited weeks to make love, and I wasn't about to cut it short with a lack of control.

He waited, though I could see the way his muscles strained to move. After a moment, when the pressure didn't seem so dangerous, I rolled my hips up, sliding deeper into him. His answering moan did nothing for my control, but neither of us slowed. I watched his body undulate as he ground his ass on my cock. His hips moved in a slow, rhythmic dance backward then forward, and his body arched gracefully even as his head fell back. Long, soft curls danced along his shoulders each time Brian drove himself onto me.

God, he was so beautiful.

I sat up as well as I could and wrapped my arms around Brian's back. His damp forehead fell onto my shoulder before he turned his head and pressed his lips to my neck. With his mouth so close to my ear, I heard every whimper. Every cry made me hold on tighter, and I never wanted it to end, even though the pulsing waves of my impending orgasm reminded me that it had to. I reached blindly to my side and felt for the bottle of lube cool against my hip. After a few distracted tries, I found it and popped the cap. Moving back a few inches, I drizzled the lube over Brian's cock as it bounced against his stomach. Slapping the bottle against my leg to close the cap, I tossed it to the side, not caring where it landed. I spread the slick liquid over Brian's erection and wrapped my hand around it as I stroked him.

"Jamie," Brian cried just before his mouth covered mine in a desperate, fevered kiss. I could feel his keening sounds just as sharply as I heard them. They made my stomach tingle with need and my cock pulse inside him. The pitch intensified as his hips moved faster. It felt like he was chasing that feeling, the one I sought to share with him. Twisting my slick fist around the head of his erection, I pushed him headlong over the edge, and he rewarded me with a cry of pure pleasure.

"I love you," I whimpered into his ear even as his ass tightened around me and hot semen pulsed from his dick, overflowing from my hand. The sentiment, coupled with the physical need, made my orgasm scream through my body and explode into the condom deep in his ass. We rode the feeling out together, our cries mingling against the backdrop of candlelight and rumpled sheets.

"Promise me that we'll always be like this," I whispered against his forehead, "that we'll always love each other like this. I can't bear the thought of being away from you ever again."

"Forever, Jamie. I will love you for the rest of my life," Brian whispered back, and then wrapped his arms around my shoulders. I held him as close as I could against my chest.

CHAPTER SIX

I RAN out of oxy three weeks later.

When Brian came home from a shoot, he found me curled up on the bathroom floor, crying. Stomach cramps had replaced the pain from the burn, causing my abdomen to feel like someone had turned it inside out. He wiped the cold sweat from my face with his palm, and I turned just in time to throw up violently in the bowl again. The cold rag he handed me felt good as I cleaned away the sweat and vomit. My head pounded, and I had a hard time trying to stand as he helped me to the bed.

"Have you been sick all day?" he asked as he set the small garbage basket from the bathroom on the floor next to the bed. I shivered under the blankets and grabbed one of the pillows to hold against my stomach as another wave of nausea rolled over me. Thankfully, that time I didn't throw up.

"Yeah," I whispered. I didn't have the energy to say more, even if the raw pain in my throat would have allowed for conversation. If I could just lay still and not move, maybe it would all stop.

Brian crawled on the bed next to me, and the motion caused my stomach to lurch again. I rolled over to the side of the bed and dry-heaved into the basket. Apparently, there was nothing left to bring up. He moved closer to me on the bed and wrapped an arm tenderly around my waist, which I immediately shrugged off. I didn't want to be touched right then; it felt like my skin was crawling.

"I'll… I'll get you something to drink from the refrigerator." His voice sounded hollow as the bed moved again, and I saw him walk toward the kitchen. I didn't have the strength or the patience to try to make him feel better. The symptoms had hit like a freight train that morning, waking me from a sound sleep. They hadn't let up all day.

Brian came back next to the bed, set down a can of lemon-lime soda, and told me that the carbonation and sugar would make me feel better.

"I'm a fucking junkie going through withdrawal. I'm sure a can of soda is going to make that right as goddamn rain," I said. I buried my head under the blanket and curled up into a tighter ball with my back to him. Just before I finally started to doze, I heard Brian talking to someone, but I couldn't focus on the words. The sound buzzed in the back of my head like a persistent fly. I wanted to tell him to shut the fuck up, but sleep pulled me under before I could.

Twenty minutes later, I was awake again and felt more tired than before I fell asleep.

"How are you feeling?"

I looked up to see Leo standing over me with Brian at his shoulder. Where Leo looked calm, but sad, Brian's face was pale. He looked almost sick. I closed my eyes, too tired to hold them open while we carried on this asinine conversation.

"Like shit," I told him honestly. Then my brain kicked in, and I remembered that Brian had been getting the oxy from Leo in the first place. Hope flared inside me. "Did you bring pills?"

"No. I wanted to get one last bag to help wean you off of them, but the dealer I'd been using was arrested last week." I rolled over away from him, feeling the darkness seep into me from every shadow in the room. He couldn't get me any more drugs, so I'd have to keep suffering for days, maybe even weeks. I had no idea how long withdrawal took, but with the way my heart kept pounding in my chest, if it went on too much longer, I'd be dead anyway.

"Then what? You came over here to watch me suffer? Why don't you sell tickets? I'm sure your buddy Mike would fucking love one. Just get the fuck out," I mumbled into my pillow because I didn't have the energy to raise my head and yell.

"Jamie!" Brian's voice sounded shocked as he admonished me. Leo stopped any kind of comment I could make.

"Brian, he's sick and in pain. Another symptom of withdrawal, along with everything else you've seen, is irritability. I've been where he is, and I know how bad he's feeling, so let's cut him some slack, okay?" Leo said quietly. "I have some things that might help a little, but he's going to have a rough time for a while." Brian finally asked the question that I needed an answer for, and I silently thanked him for it.

"How long?"

"It depends on the depth of his addiction. He's only been on the oxy for about two months, but he was already an addict before that. Generally, with the people I've seen, it's a week or two," he told Brian, and the sick feeling slammed back into me. I'd thought the worst would be over in a day or two, but I knew that if it went on longer than that, I couldn't do it. I'd always been a fucking wimp. When we first got back together, I kept saying that I'd do whatever it took to get clean for

Brian, but it was a fucking lie. I'd literally beg for something to take the edge off right then.

"He's strong, Leo. He'll make it. I'll cancel my shoots for the next week and take care of him." The conviction with which Brian spoke just made me feel worse. He had so much misplaced faith in me. I knew I would let him down; it was only a matter of when.

"What he needs right now is a roof over his head, food on the table, and stability in his life, Brian. You need to work to give him those things, not sit there and hold the bucket. Believe me, that's the last thing he wants right now. Being in the bowels of addiction, trying to crawl back out—it's humiliating. He doesn't want or need an audience," Leo said, and it sounded like he spoke from personal experience rather than watching other guys go through it. If I hadn't felt like shit right then, I'd have realized that my respect for him had grown.

"I'm sorry, I just… I feel helpless," Brian said in a small voice.

"I know, babe, but right now, this isn't about you. Go put two cups of these salts in the tub and run him a bath." I heard Brian leave the room, and I squeezed my eyes shut further.

"I don't want to take a fucking bath," I muttered even as I tried to prepare myself to get up. The blinding stomach pain had finally started to dull, but I knew if I moved, it would come back. The water started in the bathroom, and I groaned into the pillow.

"It may make you feel better, kid. The salt sometimes helps pull the toxins from your body, and it helps you relax so you can sleep." He didn't raise his voice, even to talk over the sound of the water, but I heard him. God, I wanted to sleep. Getting up and hobbling to the bathroom sounded like fucking torture, but if it meant that I could sleep afterwards, maybe it would be worth it. I kept my eyes closed and listened to the sound of the running water.

I might have dozed because then Brian was there helping me to sit up, and Leo was nowhere to be seen.

"Let's go in the bathroom—everything's ready," he said as he pushed my hair back from my forehead. As I let him pull me up, I saw that he looked sad and withdrawn. It was a minute before I realized that I'd been a dick to him earlier. Leo seemed to understand, but Brian still looked upset about it.

"I'm sorry about earlier with Leo. I know that you were trying to help me. It's just… it's hard," I told him as he wrapped one of my arms around his shoulders so that I could stand on weak legs. Steadying me with both hands on my hips, he walked behind me as I shuffled into the bathroom. I leaned against the sink as I took off the briefs and sweats I'd been wearing for two days.

"I need to take a leak. I'll be okay getting in by myself," I told him so he didn't feel the need to stand there and watch me piss. Brian took that as a dismissal and left the room without comment. I sighed, and relieved my aching bladder before crawling into the tub. The hot water relaxed my muscles, and I leaned back in the tub with my eyes closed. I had to admit that it felt nice.

After I'd been in the tub long enough for my skin to start wrinkling, I pulled the plug, stood up, and turned on the shower. I felt a little stronger than I had before being in the tub. Washing my hair and my body made me feel almost human, even though the dull pain in my stomach hadn't completely gone and I dropped the shampoo because my hands shook. I'd made it through the first day. Of course, I still had to make it through the night, but I'd take the accomplishment for what it was worth.

I dried off and wrapped the towel around my waist as I left the bathroom. Brian brought me a mug as I looked for something to wear in the small amount of clothes I'd accumulated since leaving everything at Steven's apartment.

"It's chamomile tea with a little bit of peppermint. Leo said the chamomile would help you relax, and the peppermint may help your stomach." He set the mug down on the dresser where I stood pulling on a pair of shorts over the boxers I'd found. As he turned to go, I grabbed his hand and pulled him against me. My body trembled as I held him, and he wrapped his arms tightly around me.

"Thank you," I whispered, and he put a hand on the back of my head, holding me against his shoulder.

"I'll always take care of you, Jamie," he whispered back, and we stood like that for a long time, taking comfort from each other's arms.

THE tea did help some, and I kept down the chicken soup he made for dinner—for a while, at least. When we decided to go to bed, after we'd been talking quietly on the couch for a few hours, the symptoms returned almost as strongly as they'd been that morning. Stomach pains, nausea, cold sweats, and shakes kept me on the couch when I finally made Brian go to bed. I knew there was nothing he could do for me, and he had a shoot the next day with a new studio. As much as I hated it, he needed to be at his best. Taking care of his junkie boyfriend wasn't going to help him land steady work.

Around two in the morning, the shakes tapered off, and I managed to read for a while. The soup had been lost hours before, so I munched on some crackers, trying to take the edge off my nausea. I reheated the pot of tea on the stove and returned to the little nest Brian had made for me on the couch. Propping myself on the pillows, I drank my tea and read a gay-oriented mystery novel. Until Brian had given me a virtual stack of books on his computer, I hadn't known that such things existed.

Around nine, when I'd nearly finished the second book in the series, Brian got up and made breakfast. The smell of eggs made me sick, but I had a bit of toast and bacon. The orange juice burned as it went down my raw throat, and I switched to one of the sports drinks Leo had brought the day before. He had told Brian they would help keep me from dehydrating because of all the vomiting. I didn't think that a little thirst would be all that bad compared to the rest of the shit I was going through, but I drank it to make Brian happy.

The hours swirled into each other with a haze of chills, vomiting, and the pounding of my heart. Leo checked in on me at some point, but I had no idea when that was. Most of the time, I screamed at my parents, though there was no one else in the apartment. I cursed at Steven. I was at the point of begging God to let me die when Brian came home. As he held me close on the couch, I couldn't tell if it was his sobs or my own body that made me tremble. Later, after the worst of the symptoms were over, I apologized for asking him to help me kill myself. He merely shook his head and told me he didn't want to talk about it.

Around 3:00 a.m., I fell into a fitful sleep full of dreams about Steven. I could almost feel his hands around my throat and his fists pounding my stomach. The worst part of the dream, however, came at the end, when I stood powerless as Steven taught Brian a lesson with his cock. The tears of humiliation in Brian's eyes as he took each thrust were too much for me. I woke up sobbing and retching so violently that Brian's sleepy face soon swam before my eyes, begging me to tell him what was wrong.

After that, I was too afraid to sleep again.

The third day dawned with deliberate slowness. As I sat on the edge of the bed, watching Brian sleep, I made a conscious effort to keep my breathing slow and easy despite the wild racing of my pulse. The stomach cramps had abated for the moment, but my heart constantly seemed like it wanted to leap from my chest. The anxious, pained expression, which never left Brian's face while he was awake, had relaxed in sleep. The sunlight played off his soft cherub curls, and I resisted the fierce desire to run my fingers through them.

I wanted to leave and save him from the horrors of my addiction. When he'd said that he wanted us to be together, I was sure he didn't really mean to sign up for night terrors, vomiting, and mood swings that would make a saint swear like a sailor. In fact, I think I'd even called him "Saint fucking Brian" at one point the previous night, which made my heart hurt as I watched him sleep. He tried so hard to do everything right, and I was the one who fucked it all up.

"Jamie," he whispered in his sleep. I couldn't help it. I lay down in the bed next to him and wrapped my arm around him. The gesture had more to do with comforting me than comforting him, but the result was the same. He moaned slightly in his sleep, so quietly that it was almost a sigh, and nuzzled his face into my chest. Almost as if he knew I was there, he sought my comfort.

"I love you, baby," I whispered into his hair. God, he didn't deserve what I had put him through over the last few days. He didn't deserve the yelling, cleaning up puke, or listening to me screaming in my sleep. Brian worked so hard to keep a roof over my head, feed me, and keep me safe. I turned out to be nothing more than a parasite on his life. As he snuggled closer to me and I wrapped my arms around him, a plan formed in my head.

I knew how to be what Brian needed, but first, I had to pull myself together.

"I'LL be gone most of the day. Nick wants to do some stills before we shoot. If you get hungry, I picked up a few more pizzas or there's some ham and cheese for sandwiches," Brian said as he stood at the foot of the bed with his shoes in hand. He looked gorgeous in the tight jeans and red T-shirt he'd decided on for their photo shoot this morning. I wanted to tell him that, but after three days of nearly no sleep, I couldn't get the words out. After putting on his shoes, he came to my side of the bed and sat down.

"I know this is hard, but I want you to know that I am so proud of you. You just need to hang on for a little longer," he whispered as he stroked my hair as a mother would a small child. Then, in the same fashion, he leaned down and kissed my forehead gently. As he moved away, our eyes met, and I smiled as best I could. Brian smiled back and kissed my lips gently before standing up. Once he picked up his wallet and keys from the table next to the door, he was gone.

I threw the covers back, revealing my jeans and sweatshirt, and got up. I'd showered and dressed just after dawn while Brian slept. Taking some of the cash I'd saved with Steven, I put it in my wallet and grabbed my shoes from near the door. The directions I'd written last night after putting our new address into an online mapping site would allow me to take the bus downtown.

The stomach cramps started again just as I locked the front door behind me.

"Damn it," I muttered to myself and followed the instructions, which took me to a bus stop three blocks south of our apartment. A warped-looking shelter covered in graffiti was the only indication that a bus should stop on that corner. As I stood near it, I glanced around at the boarded-up store fronts that looked like their owners had abandoned them decades before. A couple of teenagers in baggy jeans and baggier sweatshirts passed around a paper bag as they watched from the opposite curb. Without a schedule, I wasn't sure when the bus would arrive, but I didn't feel too worried in the middle of the morning.

Ten minutes after I'd gotten to the stop, a rickety bus crept to a stop near the curb, and I stepped aboard. Someone had taped a sign that read, "DRIVER CARRIES NO CHANGE," to the fare-vending thing at the top of the bus stairs.

"How much is the fare?" I asked the ancient man behind the wheel as I pulled my wallet from my back pocket. The uniform hung from his emaciated frame, and white hair spilled out over ebony skin from his matching hat. He looked as sick and frail as I felt.

"Dollar twenty-five," he said, sounding bored as he stared out of the windshield. I fed two one-dollar bills into the machine and found an empty seat near the back. Staring out the window, I watched the neighborhoods change over the next twenty minutes or so. It took far less time to reach downtown than it had to reach the apartment that first day. It seemed that Leo had taken a more scenic route to ensure that no one followed us. Soon, the buildings started to get taller, the streets and sidewalks better maintained, and the people wore more suits than hoodies.

When I started to recognize some of the areas from my time on the streets, I walked toward the front of the bus. Holding on to the handle near the bus's front door, I waited for the next stop. When he turned, and I saw the Italian café I'd stolen food from, I knew I was in the right place. The bus slowed just across from the restaurant, and as the doors opened, I got off and headed north, away from the apartment I'd shared with Steven. Coming here was a huge risk, I knew that, but I needed to get my shit together for Brian.

Tracking back through the alley, I looked down one of the side streets and saw nothing. *Damn it*. When I'd been on the streets with George, it seemed like we had to avoid a dealer on every corner, but when I needed one, they were all gone. Maybe they'd moved to different spots in the months that I'd been living with Steven. I moved down to the next block and saw the little deli where George and I had been trying to eat that night. Near the mouth of the alley, I saw two guys standing close together. One looked nervous as the other slid something into his hand. When the other man turned so that I could see his face, I remembered George pointing him out. I think he'd called the man "Tony."

Tony turned and started to head back toward the street once he'd concluded his business, and I realized I was about to miss my chance. When I hurried toward the men, the second one took off, while the dealer stood his ground.

"What, kid?" Tony asked as he searched the alley—for what, I wasn't sure. He stood about half a foot shorter than me, but with his muscular build, he probably weighed at least fifty pounds more. I wasn't a threat to him in the least, but he still looked around cautiously.

"I'm looking for some oxy," I told him quietly when I stood just a foot from him in the shadowed alley. Absently, he rubbed at the dragon tattoo on his left biceps with a dirty hand.

"Sure you are, kid. Now get lost," he said, and ran a hand over his black crew cut before turning to leave.

"No, really, please. I need it," I pleaded, and something in my voice must have resonated with him because he stopped.

"Pull up your shirt and drop your jeans to your knees," he said, and I took a step back as I realized how precarious my position was. No one knew where I'd gone, and I stood in a deserted alley with a drug dealer who'd just asked me to expose my bare skin to him.

"Why?" I asked, feeling the nausea rise in my stomach again. I'd run before I let his guy rape me—drugs or no drugs.

"Because you look like a fucking snitch, and I want to know you're not wired," he said and pushed my shoulder. I took two steps back, feeling like a complete fucking moron for what I was about to do. First, I pulled up my shirt and exposed the healing burn. The dealer didn't flinch, nor did he try to touch me. Then I let my shirt fall and unbuttoned my fly. He watched with little interest as I pulled my jeans down to my knees.

"Enough?" I asked, and jerked them back up when he nodded.

"Fine, I got sixty milligram pills going for thirty bucks a pill. How many did you want?" I had about five hundred on me, and I still needed to get back home. The math took me a minute because my fucking head screamed, and I felt fuzzy and lethargic from the withdrawal. If I got fifteen pills, that should be enough to wean myself down over a week. I still had another three hundred back at the apartment if I needed more.

"Fifteen," I said, pulled my wallet out, and counted out the four hundred and fifty for him. He shoved it in his pocket. Handing me three small bags, he took out his phone and began to type before turning to leave.

"Hey, are you usually hanging around by this deli?" I asked quickly before he turned the corner.

"Yeah, most days," he said as he put the phone back into his pocket. I walked around to the front of the deli and went inside. It was the first time I'd ever been in there, but I paid for a bottle of water and asked to use their john. The bathroom would be as good a place as any to take the oxy. My hands shook as I tried to open the bottle. I could almost taste the bitter, chalky pill even before it rested on my tongue. Saliva pooled in my mouth when I pulled the bag from my pocket. I'd start with one and see what it did for me.

It took several minutes to feel the relief start to flood my body. These pills seemed to be a higher dosage than the ones Leo had found. I closed my eyes and sank onto the toilet as the pain receded. I considered taking another one, just to counter all of the effects of the withdrawal, but I didn't want to take the chance that I couldn't make it home flying high on oxy. Taking another swig of the water, I pushed the bag of pills deep into my pocket, unlocked the stall, and headed back in the direction of the bus stop.

THE enchiladas were nearly together by the time Brian got home later that afternoon. He surprised me coming in so early, and I was suddenly glad that I hadn't wasted any time getting back to the apartment. Taking off his shoes near the door, he padded barefoot to the kitchen and gently wrapped his arms around my waist.

"Hi," he murmured against my neck while I stood with my hands buried in cheese, sauce, and browned hamburger as I assembled the remaining tortillas. I turned my head and kissed him while I coated one of the tortillas with sauce.

"I thought you were going to be late?" I asked, and sprinkled a bit of meat into the tortilla, followed by a healthy bit of cheese.

"I thought I would, but they put me up first on the schedule to shoot so I got back early. I wanted to see how you were," he admitted. "Brandon was on the schedule last, and he offered to drop me at the bus stop so I could get back home while Mike was shooting with Alex and Em."

"I wonder what Alex thought of that," I mused. We'd talked a couple of times since I'd moved into the apartment with Brian, but Alex seemed busy with his new life. I missed seeing him and talking to him, but it made me happy that he'd finally found someone who understood what an amazing guy he was, even if Mike was a dickhead.

"He thinks Em is hot, so I doubt he had a—" Brian's phone rang, interrupting his sentence. Taking it from his pocket, he looked at the display before answering. "Hey Alex, what's—" Alex's voice came through the phone with such volume that I could hear it, though I couldn't understand what he'd said. "Wait, slow down, Alex. What happened?" Brian paused as he listened to Alex, who sounded hysterical. "Hang on; I'm going to put you on speaker so Jamie can hear, too."

"He's here! Jesus, he's right outside!" Alex screamed into the phone. I could tell that he was crying, and I wanted so badly to be there to comfort him. "Mike, Em, and I were walking to the Jeep when he just came at me out of nowhere. Mike tackled him and screamed for me to run. Em pushed me toward the house, and I saw Brandon pulling up, so I ran. I'm in the… in the house, and the doors are locked. Nick called the police. Brian, what happens if—Mike!" We heard a loud clatter as Alex screamed and the phone fell. I looked at Brian, whose face had drained of color.

"Alex!" he yelled into the phone, but no one on the other end seemed to hear. "Oh my God, what if he hurt Mike? What if he got into the house?" he asked me as I washed my hands quickly in the sink. Before I could dry them, he reached out and held one. Some kind of commotion happened again on the other end of the phone.

"Hey, you there?" Mike's voice sounded tired and a little thick as he tried to talk over Alex's hysterics in the background.

"Yeah, man, are you okay?" Brian squeezed my hand and relaxed marginally.

"I'm alright—it looks worse than it is," Mike said. "I won't be able to shoot for a while, but I don't think anything's broken."

"I was so scared," Alex's voice sounded close but muffled, as if he'd buried his face in Mike's chest. I took a step closer to Brian and rested my head on his shoulder. So much suffering, and it was all because of me. I hated it.

"I was, too, to be honest," Mike admitted in a whisper I'm sure we weren't supposed to hear. "I thought he was going to get to you before we could stop him."

"We need to get you cleaned up," Alex said quietly, and for a minute, I thought Brian might hang up to give them privacy, but then Mike spoke again.

"Brian, I wanted to tell you, he knew about the oxy. I don't know how, but he said that if I didn't get out of his way that I would need it next." Mike's voice sounded strong, but shaken.

"Do you think he's watching the apartment or something?" Brian asked, and I looked over at the curtains covering the window.

"No, he kept asking where Jamie was. He couldn't know that he's there, but you guys need to be careful."

"We will," Brian assured him. "Go get cleaned up, and I'll call you tomorrow. Give Alex and Em hugs for me."

"We'll come by in a couple of days; we miss you, Brian. Stay safe," Mike said, sounding drained.

"Yeah, you too." He hit the button to disconnect and set his phone on the counter next to the dish full of assembled enchiladas. I could see the guilt in his downcast eyes, the flush of his face, and the way he curled in on himself. Pulling him against my chest, I held him.

"They went in with their eyes open, Brian. It isn't your fault," I told him as he shook slightly in my arms. Though Mike and I weren't exactly friends, I felt remorse over his injuries. The blame could never be Brian's because it would always be mine. After a minute, he started to shake his head.

"What?" I tried to make my voice as soothing as I could.

"He beat Mike enough that he's not going to be able to shoot. He could have hurt Em and Brandon, too, and we just don't know. And… and… my first thought was thank God it wasn't you. They risked themselves to protect us…. I'm so fucking selfish." Brian's voice broke, and I could say nothing to console him because, if I were completely honest with myself, that was my first thought, too. I'd said a silent word of thanks to Nick for letting Brian finish early so he wasn't there.

We stood like that for a long time, just holding each other in the kitchen until Brian grabbed a beer from the refrigerator and went to sit in the living room while I put the food in the oven. Though I was sorry that Mike was hurt, especially since it made Alex worry, I was thankful that the circumstances distracted Brian from the fact that I wasn't suffering anymore, even though the guilt and the fear still ate at me. I couldn't understand how Steven knew about the oxy. I hated the thought that he'd beat someone up at the studio to get information about me, or that he'd been watching Leo. The dealer I scored from couldn't have known anything because I never mentioned my name or anything.

Brian didn't really talk during dinner, his mind miles away with Mike and Alex. I wanted to tell him to get on the bus and go stay the night at the boarding house so that he could see Mike's injuries for himself, but I couldn't force myself to be so selfless. I didn't want Brian anywhere near the boarding house now that Steven had gone on the offensive. The thought scared the fuck out of me. If Steven knew about the oxy, he might also know about Brian.

Goddamn it, I was sick of being scared all the time.

Soft, sweet lips moved over the back of my neck as I stood at the sink rinsing dishes to put them in the machine. When Brian's arms went around me, his hands rested on my chest, and for a little while, I felt whole. My arms ached to turn around and comfort him, but guilt stopped me from doing so because the comfort would ultimately be mine, and I didn't deserve it. I disengaged from Brian for just a second to finish putting the last few pieces in the machine, add soap, and turn it on. When I finished, Brian turned me so that I faced him.

"How are you feeling, honey?" As he asked, against the skin of my cheek, he traced the contour of my jaw with light kisses. I loved the feeling of his fingers ghosting over my back just beneath the hem of my T-shirt.

"My stomach is kind of iffy, but I feel okay right now." I didn't want to tell him that the problem with my stomach stemmed more from the Mexican food than the withdrawal, but he didn't ask me to elaborate.

"Will you come and lay down with me for a while?" His voice trembled as he asked, still upset over the call from Mike. He needed me, and I could not find it in myself to deny him. When I nodded, his mouth closed over mine and took it in a tender kiss. Taking my hand, he led me to the bed and we climbed in, still fully dressed. As soon as my head hit the pillow, I opened my arms because I knew what he needed. The grateful expression on his face warmed me, and when his head rested on my shoulder, I tightened my arms around him.

"Thanks," he whispered, and I kissed the wild brown curls beneath my lips. The feeling of his hand on my chest went straight to my heart, and I cherished that connection with him. No matter what went wrong in my life, his touch made everything better.

It didn't take long before holding turned to touching, and touching turned to kissing. Careful of the lingering pain in my abdomen, he rolled almost on top of me and tangled his legs with mine when the kissing became more intense. Tilting his head, he brought our lips together over and over, each time deepening the contact. Our tongues danced in an erotic expression of emotion as Brian forced his guilt and upset to the surface. It burned away in a fiery explosion of need. Quick panting breaths punctuated our long open-mouthed kisses, and his moan vibrated against my lips. The way he sucked my bottom lip between his own set my body aflame.

Not bothering to undress me, Brian unbuttoned my jeans, pulled my briefs down beneath my balls, and plunged my hardening cock into his mouth. Being blown while still almost fully clothed seemed like a sin, but his mouth felt like heaven. The way he relaxed between my spread legs on the bed, his body didn't touch me anywhere except where his lips stroked up and down my dick.

The drugs in my system relaxed me and made it difficult for me to hold off. I wanted to touch him too, but he had other plans. Most likely, because of his guilt over Mike, he felt desperate to make someone else feel good. His teeth scraped my sensitive skin and my back arched in response. A low moan vibrated around my cock, and I looked down to see Brian unbuttoning his own jeans. It turned me on when he got so excited by blowing me that he needed to stroke his own dick.

"Baby, that feels… incredible," I told him and slid cool fingers along my chest to pull and pinch hard nipples. Lost in the perfect arousal his mouth caused, I chased the tingle racing through my groin. Again and again, he tightened his lips around my shaft, sucking hard as his mouth slid toward the head. I couldn't help but to fist his hair in a desperate need to hold on to something.

The smacking of his lips as he sucked me just made my arousal that much hotter.

"Oh fuck…. Oh God…." My moans grew louder when his head bobbed faster and he tried to push me over that final line toward a hot orgasm, made even better because Brian made it happen. My ass clenched, and I wished my stomach felt better, but it seemed as though intercourse was off the table for us. Instead, I focused on the way my cock slid in and out of his mouth.

Spreading my legs farther apart, he pressed my knees to the bed, and I tried in vain to lift my hips and go deeper into his mouth. My orgasm felt so close, and my mouth watered as I thought about sucking him in return.

"Come on, baby, I want to taste you," he muttered in a low, breathless voice as he released my dick for just a moment before my body locked, each muscle going taut with the strain of my explosive release. He stayed with me, teasing out every bit of my come by sucking lightly on the head of my dick. Just when I thought I couldn't take any more, I felt him groan around me in his mouth, and I knew he'd just shot his load on the bed.

I let my head fall back onto the pillow and tried to catch my breath as he pulled back and rested his temple against my thigh. He left a small secret kiss on my naked hip, and I moved down in the bed as he moved up. Our mouths met in the middle, and I kissed him hard and tasted my own semen in his mouth.

Collapsing in my arms, Brian whispered his love for me, and the guilt returned with gale force.

When Brian went to take a shower, I grabbed the bag of pills hidden in the empty battery compartment of a radio we never used. I'd never felt more like an addict than I did right then. I might as well have been hiding in an alley shooting up. Pushing that thought away, I took two of the pills because I needed that fucking oblivion. Brian might notice something, but we wouldn't be up too much longer anyway. The oxy would help me finally fucking sleep. I hadn't slept in days, and I needed it so badly.

MIKE'S injuries ended up being worse than he'd thought, and during the night Alex took him to an emergency care center. They didn't keep him, probably because—like the rest of us—he had no insurance, but they did put six stitches in his face. Alex wanted him to stay with us or with Brandon, but he refused to leave. Leo installed a deadbolt on the door leading to the second floor, as well as on the back door of the building, because he was sure Steven would think they'd hidden me there.

Brian and Alex canceled their shoots with Hartley for that next month, picking up work with other studios. It disappointed Mike that Alex had booked a few out of town shoots, but he knew it would be better for Alex. He diligently drove Alex back and forth to the airport whenever he needed to go.

I'd managed to make the pills last for almost two weeks by taking only one a day, but whenever I tried to stretch it to more than one day between pills, I felt just like I had that very first day of withdrawal. If I went into withdrawal again, Brian would know that I'd been using. He'd been so proud of me for "beating my addiction." Of course, he had no idea I hadn't beaten it at all. With everything else he'd gone through over Steven, I couldn't lay that on him too.

We hadn't had sex since the night we'd celebrated his birthday. I couldn't even look him in the eye, much less make love to him. He hadn't mentioned it, but I knew it bothered him. It felt like things were closing in on me. Brian knew something was bothering me. I'd run out of pills the day before, and if I didn't go back to the dealer, Brian would know he still slept every night with a fucking junkie. Saint Brian was so fucking brave and noble, he wouldn't understand just how much of a coward *his* Jamie had become.

"Babe, it's seven. Don't you have a shoot today?" I asked as I shook Brian awake the next morning. My pulse raced because without the hit of oxy I normally had every morning, the withdrawal symptoms would start again. I should have gone downtown yesterday to make sure I didn't run out, but I knew it would be safer for me to go when Brian had a shoot.

"Oh, hey, Trevor called last night from Lawnboys.com. They had to cancel," Brian said and rolled over to pull me into bed with him. I couldn't think for the panic. Without that pill, I'd be very sick soon, and Brian would know. My brain worked furiously as he began to kiss my neck. He moaned softly against my skin.

"I missed this," he whispered, moving down my bare chest. The kiss of his warm breath against my skin made me shiver as cold sweat trickled down the back of my neck. I tried to focus on the feeling of his lips, but the nausea, which had started with my guilt, grew as he licked a line across my abs just above my navel. I sat up quickly and moved back to sit against the headboard, out of his reach. The look of hurt on his face took my guilt to a completely new level.

"I'm sorry. I just don't feel well," I explained, and for the first time in nearly a month, my excuse happened to be true. "My stomach is killing me."

"Sure." He picked at a loose thread on the comforter to avoid my eyes. When I didn't move or speak, he looked up. At the sadness in his face, I nearly confessed. I couldn't stand seeing that devastated expression. Then I thought about what kind of expression he would wear if I told him that I was still an addict and that I'd gone downtown just a few blocks from Steven's apartment to score, and I stayed quiet.

"Honestly, Brian—" I started, but he cut me off.

"Is it because I'm still doing porn?" he asked in a small voice. "Is that why you don't want me?" My stomach lurched painfully before I could answer him, and I jumped off the bed and ran for the bathroom. I didn't even have time to close the door before I threw up violently. A hand rubbed my back as I bent over the bowl and waited to see if anything else would come up.

"Oh God, Jamie, I'm sorry," Brian said as he stepped out of the tiny bathroom. I heard the hall closet open, and he came back with a washrag, which he wet in the sink and then laid on the back of my neck. It felt good, and I stayed hunched for several minutes until I felt confident that the worst had passed. Taking the rag off my neck, I wiped my face and then sat on the bathroom floor with my back against the wall.

"We've talked about the porn, Brian. I accept that you have to do it so that we can survive. I'd be pretty fucking shitty to hold that over you when it feeds me and keeps a roof over my head," I said as I rocked lightly and held my stomach. The cramps were worse than they had been the last time. Sweat poured down my face, and I wiped it away with the rag still clutched in my hand.

"I'm sorry," Brian whispered.

"It's okay," I said. "I know I haven't been myself lately. I'm just working out some shit in my head. It's not your fault I'm so messed up, Brian."

"Any idea what made you so sick?" he asked as he sat on the floor with his back against the small tub. I put my arms around my knees and then rested my forehead on them. Of course, I knew exactly what had made me sick, but I had no idea what to tell him. It couldn't be food poisoning because we'd eaten the exact same thing for dinner last night.

"Maybe you have the stomach flu. I should call my dad and see if there's anything we can do," he said. When I finally looked up at him, he watched me with careful eyes. I didn't know what he suspected, but without the pills, he couldn't prove anything. When he went out tomorrow to work, I'd go see the dealer and get another dozen pills and finish weaning myself off the drugs. If I could just get down to half a pill a day, that would make it easier.

"I think I'm going to lie down for a while." My voice sounded loud in the small room. I thought I might vomit again as I struggled to get to my feet.

"I'm going down to the gas station on the corner to pick up some of those fruit punch sports drinks you like." He stood up, too, and put a hand on my back as I stumbled to the bed.

It turned out to be a really long day.

THE next day, I rose before the sun as I had done so often. Sitting on the living room couch with the rest of my savings stashed in my pocket, I cradled an untouched cup of coffee in my cold hands. My stomach rolled and my hands shook as I waited for Brian to get up and leave for his shoot. I didn't have the energy to get off the couch and take a shower. The fucking dealer would have to take me unshaven and without a shower, though I'm sure he'd seen much worse.

Around nine thirty, just when I'd given up hope on him ever getting up, he rolled over and patted my side of the bed. I loved that he was looking for me even though I wasn't there. After a few minutes of disorientation, he sat up, looked at me, and flopped back down onto his pillow.

"Why are you all the way over there?" he asked. Sleep muffled his voice, and I had to smile at how sweet and sexy he sounded. Despite how awful I felt, I went to him and sat on the side of the bed. He sighed—a happy, relaxed sound—as he ran his hand up and down my back.

"Is this better?" I rested a hand on his chest.

"Much better," he admitted. "How are you feeling, baby?"

"Better," I lied. "While you're at your shoot, I think I'll just hang out on the couch and maybe try to eat some soup." My stomach lurched both at the guilt of lying to Brian and the thought of food. When my hand started to shake on his chest, I stood up. "It's almost ten. What time do you have to be at the studio?"

"Uh, I think I have to be there by eleven thirty. Can you hand me my phone?"

I looked around for a minute and then spotted the smartphone sitting on the table in front of the couch. I weaved drunkenly as I maneuvered around the end of the bed but found my balance on the way to the living room. I didn't think Brian noticed since he'd buried his head in the blankets.

"Yeah, I have to be there at eleven thirty. They want to get some stills before the shoot," he said with a yawn after I handed him the phone. "I should get up. Did you have breakfast?"

"Mmhmm," I said, trying not to completely lie to him.

"Okay, I'll throw something together and then get in the shower," he decided aloud. I went into the living room and tried to think of how I could avoid the smell of food.

An hour later, Brian mercifully left for his shoot, and I followed about twenty minutes later so that we didn't run into each other at the bus stop. The ride downtown felt longer than it had the last time, maybe because I had a better idea of what to expect, and I just wanted to get it over with. The bus didn't have a bathroom, so I had to force myself to wait until I found a convenience store downtown in order to throw up. Things couldn't go on as they were. I could not come back downtown for drugs again. With every bit of will I could muster, I promised myself that these last pills would be enough to break my addiction.

I reached the deli behind which the dealer did his business. At first, I panicked because I didn't see any sign of him, but then I turned the corner into the alley and watched as he fought with some other poor soul who had no money for the shit that he needed. The junkie wore jeans that had to be at least three sizes too big, probably from the weight he'd lost to the drugs. A peeling, undecipherable design covered his ratty black tank top. The dirt caked into it made me think maybe he'd been rolling around on the ground, and bruises on his arms lent credence to the idea. Grease coated his unkempt black hair, and it was obvious he hadn't seen a razor in quite a while. I wondered, if Brian hadn't saved me, would I have turned out like that battered man?

The dealer pushed the junkie and told him to fucking get lost. My heart ached a little for the man, who begged for something, anything, to get him through the day. When the dealer pulled his arm back to punch the guy, the junkie cowered away from the blow and scampered out of the alley.

"What the fuck do you want?" the dealer asked, and I took a step closer.

"Do you still have sixty milligram tabs of oxy?" I tried to stop my voice from cracking as I asked, but was unsuccessful. He looked me up and down for a minute.

"No, I have eighties," he replied, looking bored. He pulled a phone out of his pocket and started typing, as if I weren't standing in front of him trying to conduct business. Damn it, the eighty milligram pills would be more expensive, and I didn't have a lot of cash as it was.

"How much?"

"They're a buck per milligram," he said as a text came through his phone, and he put it back in his pocket. At eighty dollars a pill, I'd only be able to afford four pills. They were a higher dosage, but I'd planned to leave with ten. My breathing accelerated, and I felt the rolling in my stomach start again. I did a little mental math and took a deep breath, hoping the focus would keep my voice from shaking.

"A couple weeks ago, they were fifty cents per milligram. What the fuck happened since then?" I asked, stalling for time so that I could think. I still had my key to Steven's apartment. I could get in there and get my stuff to try to sell, but I'd be fucked if he caught me.

"The cost of shit changes all the time, kid. Do you want them or not?"

"I...." With a deep sigh, I surrendered to the inevitable. I'd just have to cut these pills in half and make do. "I'll take four."

"Four? That's it?" he asked, and I heard the skepticism in his voice.

"That's all I've got the cash for," I admitted and started to pull the money from my pocket. He looked at me again, differently that time, as if he were trying to make a decision. His brow furrowed below his receding hairline, and he checked his phone again.

"Maybe we can work something out," he said after a few minutes and ran a single finger down the front of my shirt. With some difficulty, I repressed a shiver of revulsion.

"Like what?" I almost didn't want to know as a fiery gleam came into his eyes. I'd seen that gleam before in Steven's eyes. Sex usually followed closely after. "I'm not fucking you."

"I'll give you ten pills for three hundred and a blow job," he offered, and ran a thick finger across my lower lip. "I bet you give fantastic head." The tattoo on his biceps danced as I slapped his hand away. "Hey, you want four instead of ten, that's fine with me." He reached into his pocket, and I panicked. Four wouldn't be enough to get me through my addiction. I didn't understand why I'd hesitated. I mean, I'd sucked off guys for a living when I lived with Steven. I'd done porn to pay off a drug debt, so there was really no fucking difference. Brian's face swam before my eyes, but I pushed it away. I couldn't think of him right then.

Tears welled in my eyes as I pulled my wallet out of my back pocket and grabbed the condom hidden in its folds. Keeping my eyes on the dirty alley beneath my feet, I slowly sank to my knees.

CHAPTER SEVEN

THE steamy shower wasn't hot enough to wash away my feelings of self-disgust. I slid down the wall to sit on the floor of the tub as the water pelted me in the face. It would never make me clean. I'd just whored myself out for drugs; I'd never be clean again.

Brian came home while I sat in the shower trying to come to terms with what I'd done. I heard his cheerful voice through the curtain telling me how Mike was looking better and how Alex had decided to put up a blog. I didn't care about any of it, but I made the appropriate noises anyway. When he asked if he could join me, I nearly threw up at the thought of putting my mouth on him after where it had been earlier. I told him that the water had started to turn cold and I was getting out anyway.

"I don't feel like cooking tonight. How's your stomach feeling? Are you up for Chinese?" he asked, and I agreed. Whatever he wanted, I didn't care. Maybe Steven had been right—I didn't deserve to make choices for myself because I always made the wrong ones.

I told him to order whatever he wanted and turned off the water. It took several minutes for me to find the energy to stand up and grab a towel. Standing with my back against the bathroom door, I heard Brian call through the door that the food would be there in about twenty minutes. Hearing the joy and love in his voice was pure torture. I didn't deserve any of it. I didn't deserve him.

Finally, I wrapped the towel around my waist and walked over to the dresser to grab something to wear. I grabbed the first two things I found that halfway matched and put them on over a pair of briefs. Nothing mattered to me right then—not food, clothes, or even the drugs I'd hidden in the bottom of my underwear drawer. My heart broke with guilt, and I wished I could take everything back and just tell Brian the truth about my addiction.

"Come sit with me," Brian said from the couch and held out his arms. The very least I could do was sit in his arms and make him happy. I owed him so much, and all I ever repaid him with was grief. Sitting on the edge of the couch next to Brian, I pulled on the socks I'd carried with me and then settled into his arms. It made things even worse. His comfort and his love were like acid to me right then, burning my skin until I wanted to scream. When he whispered in my ear that he loved me, I couldn't stop the sobs that broke from my chest. Once I told him what I'd done, our relationship would be over. After he'd worked so hard for us to be together, my betrayal would be the last straw, and I couldn't blame him at all. I was a selfish prick, caring more about the drugs than I did him, only thinking about myself, and I deserved to be alone.

"Jamie, baby, what's wrong?" he asked with that same patient love that I always heard in his voice, which made me sob harder because soon I'd never hear it again. I shook my head, unable to speak. Wrapping his hand around the back of my neck, he pulled my head onto his shoulder and held me. The scent of him filled me with memories of happier times, and I threw my arms around his shoulders and clung to him. He seemed to be at a loss, because he simply patted my back lightly.

After a while, the sobs subsided to hiccup-punctuated cries. I owed it to him to tell him the truth, and deep down I knew I needed to tell him, but I couldn't find the words.

"Please, we can't fix it if we don't talk about it," he whispered, so I sat up and wiped my eyes. I'd been hiding things from him for weeks, and I couldn't do it anymore. I wiped my eyes as someone knocked on the door.

"It's the food. We are going to talk about this," he warned as he unlocked the door and pulled his wallet out of his back pocket.

Even with his training and reflexes, Brian couldn't dodge the fist that came at him fast enough. When he fell backward through the door, slamming it against the wall, I watched in horror as Steven stepped over the threshold. His long black hair and malevolent sneer were just as I remembered, but he seemed larger than life as he kicked Brian, who hadn't made it to his feet.

"Stop it!" I screamed, the tears making my hoarse voice crack. Brian got to his feet just as I did and backed up to give himself room. He didn't say anything—he just waited for the next attack. When Steven charged at him, he landed two blows to Steven's face and a solid kick to his head. His body hit the floor with a dull thud, and I came forward, intending to help, but Brian waved me off. Steven struggled to get up from his knees, glaring at Brian. Even with all our fights, I'd never seen him wear such a murderous expression. Blood trickled from Steven's nose and split lip. He wiped them away absently as he watched Brian ready himself for another attack.

As Steven took another step toward Brian, I saw my greatest fear tucked in the back of his belt.

"Brian, he has a gun!" The shout had barely left my throat when Steven grabbed me around the neck and held me against his chest. He pulled the weapon from his waistband and jammed it against my head. The cold metal of the barrel pressed into my temple, and Brian froze with his hands held up in front of him. My heart stopped at the fear and desperation in his eyes.

"Hey, man, let's just calm down and talk about this," Brian said, and I had to envy his composure because, right then, I was fucking terrified. I had no idea if Steven would shoot me. It didn't seem as if he would since he'd tried so hard to find me and bring me back. If it had to be one of us, I prayed silently that Steven would shoot me instead of hurting Brian. I knew I'd never be able to survive if he took the only thing in my life that mattered to me.

"There's nothing to fucking talk about. You took my boy, and I'm here to take him back," Steven said, and the chill in his voice made me shiver. I had no doubt that he would kill Brian if either of us resisted. I refused to give him the chance.

"I'll go with you. Please, just don't hurt him," I told Steven even as Brian protested. Brian took a step forward, and Steven pointed the gun at him instead.

"You'd beg for his life? I could be dying in the street and you'd step over me. What is so fucking special about him? Who the fuck is he, anyway, your high school sweetheart?" His voice chilled my blood as he whispered in my ear. I had to get him out of the apartment before something horrible happened.

"Please," I pleaded again. "Let's just go home, Steven, please." At the mention of the word home, Steven held me closer to him. It seemed he didn't care if I loved him, only if I belonged to him. Brian tensed at what he must have mistaken for a display of affection. Steven's harsh chuckle against my ear scared me.

"Jamie, shut up," Brian insisted. "I'm not going to just let you leave with him." Damp lips pressed against my cheek as Steven kissed me and readjusted his grip on the gun. I felt his heavy breaths on my skin. Time seemed to stop as we each waited for someone else to break the tension, which had crept into the room like a fog. Terrified even to breathe, I trembled in Steven's arms.

Brian turned his attention to Steven.

"Look, no one needs to get hurt here, just let Jamie come to me and you can leave. We won't call the police." Brian reached for me, and Steven jerked me backward hard by my neck.

"God, you really have no fucking clue, do you?" Steven asked him, his voice full of sarcasm. "Do you want to know how I found you?" In that moment, I realized my fatal mistake and wished he would shoot me rather than finishing the thought. Of course dealers, especially ones around his apartment, would know Steven. He had tons of pictures of me from Hartley. What better way to find a junkie than have dealers watching for him. I'd walked right into his arms and led him to Brian. If I had been honest with Brian, none of it would have happened.

Brian didn't answer; he merely tried to reassure me with his gentle gaze.

"Steven, let's just go," I said and tried to pull out of his grasp so I could get him out the door, not caring what happened after that.

"No, no... I think that he should know what kind of piece of shit he risked his life for. You see, I found you because lover boy here used one of my dealers to score today, and I had Tony follow him to see where he was living. Unfortunately, since the little fuck hasn't been working lately, he fell a little short on cash. So, he made up the difference by getting down on his knees in an alley and sucking Tony off. It's good to know he hasn't lost his touch."

Brian's face drained of color, and I could see that he was about to argue when he searched my face for answers. I couldn't look him in the eye, and that must have confirmed what he needed to know because he didn't dispute what Steven had said. When I finally got the balls to look up, I saw every ounce of pain and betrayal in his defeated posture and tear-filled eyes.

"He wouldn't have needed the drugs if you hadn't beaten the fuck out of him!" Brian screamed as a tear rolled down his cheek, and he took a step forward, raising his fist. The blast from the gun was deafening in the small apartment. I watched in stunned disbelief as Brian stumbled backward, a red stain blossoming through his white T-shirt.

"Brian!" I sobbed as the scream ripped through me. Brian looked up at me. I could see his eyes were wide and shocked even as he started to stumble sideways toward the couch. "No…. No, Brian… please!" I fought against Steven's hold, trying desperately to get to Brian, who had fallen to his knees. Blood poured into the front of his shirt. Steven picked me up off my feet to stop me from getting out of his grasp, but I fought anyway. I had to get to Brian. I had to call an ambulance. Jesus, there was so much blood.

The butt of the gun slammed into the base of my skull, causing colored lights to pop in front of my eyes. The pain didn't register at first, but as darkness closed around me, the last thing I saw was Brian's head bouncing off our living room floor as he collapsed.

"JAY.... Come on, Jay, wake up for me, baby." The blinding pain in my head took all of my focus for several minutes. My moan sounded piteous as it bounced around the inside of my sore skull. I tried to touch the back of my head, just above my neck, but something cold pressed against the spot where most of the pain radiated from. Confused and disoriented, I just sat with my eyes closed and tried to figure out why my head hurt so goddamned badly. The fingers in my hair distracted me only slightly from the pain, but they felt nice so I leaned into them.

"Babe, can you hear me?" Recognition finally penetrated the pain, and my eyes popped open to find Steven watching my face. I scrambled back against the couch in the little room I recognized as his basement office in the apartment building. As my consciousness returned, I remembered the shocking events that led to me being with him. *Brian.* I forced myself to calm down and think.

"Please, I'll stay with you. Just let me call an ambulance for Brian. Please, I won't tell anyone. He's hurt, and...." My plea died in my throat when I saw fear in his face as he shook his head slowly. I'd never seen Steven O'Dell scared of anything.

"Jay, you've been out for hours. He's... he's dead, baby." His voice shook as he spoke. I looked around the office, trying to find anything that would prove him wrong. Brian couldn't be dead. He couldn't. I searched my memory and found that last horrifying moment before Steven had knocked me out. In perfect, sickening clarity, I watched the blood seeping through Brian's shirt. I saw the look of shock and fear on his face. I stared in speechless disbelief as he fell.

"No... no.... You can't.... He couldn't...." I spluttered as my stomach rolled, and Steven grabbed a plastic bin just in time for me to throw up. Hoarse, broken sobs followed, and I didn't even try to stop them. My Brian, my beautiful Brian died trying to save me. I couldn't stand the pain that caused. The self-hatred and loathing would come in time, but for then, I succumbed to the grief of losing the man I loved more than anything else in the world. My head pounded as I cried, and I welcomed it. I deserved the pain. I deserved so much worse. It should have been me lying there in a pool of blood, alone and scared after being shot like a dog.

"Please don't cry. You're only going to make yourself sick. Let's just go upstairs," Steven pleaded and seemed to be at a loss about how to deal with my reaction. It took a long time for me to calm down. Each time that I thought the tears had stopped, I'd see Brian's face in my mind and they'd start again. The bastard watched me as I cried, and I wondered if he took joy from it. The idea that he enjoyed my pain allowed me to pull myself together, wipe off my face, and stand up. Pulling my arm from his grasp when he tried to help, I let him lead me through the lobby to the elevator. My legs were numb, and Steven kept his arm around my waist to steady me as we walked. His touch should have repulsed me, but I just didn't care. My love lay dead on the floor of our apartment, and I felt like I'd died with him.

When we reached the apartment, Steven opened the door and pulled me through into his arms. The living room, the kitchen—nothing had changed. I could have been coming back from a shoot as if the last several weeks had never happened. Then, at least, Brian would still be alive.

"Why don't you go lay down for a while, Jay?" Steven suggested as he steered me toward the bedroom. I guessed that meant I didn't have to sleep on the couch anymore, as I had when Brian and his friends intervened. Not even bothering to take off my shoes, I crawled on top of the perfectly made bed and rested my head on the pillow as I stared at the wall. Steven lay down behind me, flush against my back, and wrapped his arm around my waist. I forced myself not to shiver in revulsion at his touch. Instead, I concentrated on the dead feeling making its way through me. The shock had turned into numbness, which I found soothing just then.

"I missed you so much, Jamie," he said after a few minutes. "I know that you got scared after we fought that last time, and I'm so sorry I hurt you." It surprised me how little he really understood me after living with me for so long. Either he was deliberately obtuse, or he had missed quite a few social lessons in his formative years. "Things are going to be different this time, baby. I promise. I'm going to do everything I can to make you happy. From now on, it's just you and me. No more porn and no more photo shoots because I'm going to take really good care of you." I didn't say anything. I didn't have to. He'd made up his mind. Things would happen according to his plan, and I'd go along with it because I didn't have anything to live for anyway. Without Brian, I had nothing.

We stayed in bed for another hour as he whispered promise after promise in the growing darkness. After a while, he gave me two oxy he'd gotten from the dealer and went to order food. Since I no longer had any shame, I took them both with the water he'd brought from the bathroom sink and welcomed the fog of oblivion.

"JAMIE, you need to wake up, baby." Steven's voice sounded loud and frantic in my semi-conscious state. "Come on, stand up." He pulled on my arm, and I sat up on the edge of the bed. Bright sunlight filtered in through the curtains, and I realized the drugs had kept me out through the night and into the next day. As he pulled me to my feet, my brain kicked in a little better, and I understood that Steven was panicked.

"What?" I asked as he threw my shoes at me and opened the front door.

"Go down the hall and around the corner until the cops come into the apartment. Then, go downstairs and across the street to the coffee shop. Take this." He handed me a fifty and my wallet as he pushed me barefoot into the hall. I considered going straight to the elevator, waiting for the cops, and telling them everything. I even took a few steps in that direction before I remembered that the police had never been able to hold Steven on anything. He'd been arrested for drugs, violence, and a host of other charges just in the few months we'd been together, but he always came back. If I talked against him, and he walked away from it, he was capable of anything. I'd watched him murder my best friend, and Alex could very well be the next person on his list if I didn't do exactly what he wanted me to do.

So, instead of trying to find justice for my Brian, I let him down again by turning around and hiding as I was told.

The elevator doors were loud in the otherwise silent hallway. I couldn't see the police officers, and their shoes made no noise on the carpeting as they walked toward the apartment. Only low voices gave away their presence.

"You see how fast that doorman got on the phone. I bet he already knows we're here," a husky, quiet voice said. I could tell it was a man, but I couldn't get any other ideas about the speaker from it.

"He's a person of interest for right now, but he's been arrested so many times, I'm sure he knows the drill." Another voice, slightly higher, replied. That voice sounded older, kind of like Leo's voice. A sharp pang went through me at the thought of Leo. I wondered if he knew about Brian yet. He had to. Mike, Alex, and Emilio probably all knew by then. My heart ached, and I wondered how they'd told Richard and Carolyn.

A loud knocking brought me out of my thoughts, and I held my breath while I waited for Steven to answer. I reached down and started to put on my shoes because I wanted to be able to hit the elevator as soon as they went in.

"Can I help you?" Steven's voice sounded calm as he talked to the officers. In fact, he sounded almost bored. I heard the rustling of clothing, and then the lower-voiced cop spoke.

"My name is Detective Neilson, and this is my partner, Detective Roberts. We're investigating a shooting in the area. Would you mind if we came in to speak with you?" I closed my eyes and balled my hands into fists as I waited for his response.

"I'd be happy to help if I can. Please, come in," Steven announced, and I heard more movement. The door closed, so I peeked around the corner to make sure everyone had gone into the apartment. When I was satisfied they were gone, I crept to the elevator. The apartment door didn't open, and no one stopped me as I made my way to the lobby.

The coffee shop across the street where Steven had told me to go was deserted. I crawled into a booth in the back and waited. After a few minutes, a middle-aged waitress with hot pink earrings and a vacant expression asked me what I wanted. Without giving it too much thought, I asked for a soda. I didn't want anything to eat, but I knew I needed to order something if I wanted to wait for Steven. He hadn't given me any keys, so I was stuck there until he came to get me.

It took nearly forty-five minutes, during which time I had to order a lunch special so that the waitress would stop giving me looks. I ate maybe a quarter of the sandwich and a few chips before I pushed it away. Restless and irritable, I didn't want the rest of the fucking sandwich. I just wanted for whatever was going on upstairs to be over. If they were going to arrest him, or if they were going to let him get away with murder, I couldn't stand the wait. Steven finally strolled in, and his smug smile told me everything I needed to know.

He dropped down into the booth across from me and grabbed a menu, totally at ease with the world.

ONE part of Steven's promise that first night turned out to be true. He made a real effort to make life with him different since he'd brought me back. During those first few weeks, he never hit me or threw things at me. He never even raised his voice. He sighed a lot, so I could tell my lack of enthusiasm or involvement in our relationship frustrated him, but he didn't show it with violence. Steven had also not pressed me for sex, which surprised me, though I was sure it wouldn't be too much longer before he forced the issue. Since I didn't work, he supported me, and I'm sure he figured sex went with the whole domestic-life package.

One of my worst days with Steven came about three days after Brian's death when I realized that they would probably have some kind of service for him. I begged Steven to let me call Alex to find out the details, but he simply unplugged the house phones and took them to his office in the basement. Alex probably hated me anyway. I'd gotten Brian killed out of a selfish need to get high. Mike must feel vindicated. I had been the worst choice Brian made with his life.

The police had returned twice since the day he'd pushed me out into the hall barefoot and told me to hide. Each time, he made sure that the police never saw me, but I couldn't tell if he hid me from them, or if he hid them from me. He certainly didn't trust me to speak with them, so he made sure they couldn't find me. To ensure they didn't come up when he was working, he left strict instructions with the desk to let them up only when he was home and to call him if they showed up. They always came in the evenings, however, so he never had to worry.

For me, each day melded into the next with terrifying slowness. Each one that I survived brought me that much closer to death. In death, maybe I could escape the suffocating guilt that drowned me during my waking hours. The nights were no better. Every time I closed my eyes, I saw Brian's bloody body and his wide, accusing eyes. I watched the shock and pain distort his perfect face into a terrifying mask.

After a while, I stopped sleeping. I spent mornings and evenings drinking coffee and wandering listlessly through the apartment. I cooked, I cleaned, and I did laundry. Anything I found to keep my time occupied so that I could stay awake, I did. At night, when we lay side by side in Steven's king-sized bed, I simply stared at the wall and tried hard not to think of Brian. Sometimes, I read while he slept, but when the light bothered him, he made me turn it off. The lack of sleep, in combination with the drugs he fed me, made me feel disconnected from my life. It reminded me of those old movies where an alien took over someone's body. I felt like someone had taken over mine, and I spent my days going through the motions.

One of my few jobs was to put together a grocery list. I sat on the couch, listlessly staring at the notebook paper, which Steven would then use to place an order with an online service that delivered the groceries. It had been weeks since I'd left the apartment. I made the list, but only to have something to do. Caught in limbo between life and death, I never stepped out of line. I never even thought about calling Alex or Leo at the boarding house anymore to see how they were coping without Brian because I couldn't risk Steven's anger with any of us. Brian found out the hard way what happens when you make him angry.

Listing the ingredients for several Mexican dishes, I pulled myself off the couch to go see if we actually had any of the things we needed. I didn't much care either way, but it gave me something to do. Pulling each of the cabinet doors open, one at a time, I found a few of the spices I'd need, but little else. As I put the cumin back on the shelf, it slipped from my fingers and crashed to the floor. When I lived with

Steven before, that kind of mistake would have terrified me, but I couldn't muster any sort of response. Instead, I just grabbed the broom and dustpan so I could sweep up the broken container and spilled spice.

The methodical cleaning reminded me of the night I'd spent scrubbing the floor on my hands and knees, my stomach burning with more pain than I'd ever felt in my life. Hatred flared in my heart, and while I knew it wasn't productive, I let it fester there. In that moment, I really couldn't decide whom I hated more—Steven or myself.

Once I deposited the debris from the broken bottle into the garbage, I put the broom back into the small closet and threw the dustpan in behind it. I heard a dull thud as a box near the bottom of the closet fell over. I sighed and picked it up, noticing a fine white powder that trickled from an open corner near the top. I swept the little bit of pooled rat poison into the dustpan and dumped it into the garbage can. The consistency of the powder reminded me of coke. As I dropped the dustpan, I felt a detached fascination with the comparison. In the last John Marshall novel I'd read, the lawyer had paid someone to lace a witness's coke to kill him so he couldn't testify against the lawyer's client.

I stared at the box in my hand. It would be the perfect way to stop the pain. If I mixed the poison with my coke the next time he fed me drugs, then it would be over. Steven would finally have no more power over me. No one would have any power over me. I could be free. As I took a moment to think about what it would be like, I wondered what Steven would do. He could go after one of my friends, but that wasn't likely, not if I were gone. More realistically, he'd probably find another boy and go on about his life. Steven would find him while he was at his most vulnerable and then ruin his life.

Anger snaked its way up into my chest, and I knew that I couldn't let that happen either. I couldn't let him destroy someone else just to save myself. The answer was simple, and I felt no fear as I carried the box into the bedroom, hoping that Steven hadn't moved his personal stash of coke.

WHEN Steven came home about half an hour later, I met him at the door with a smile. He smiled back and tentatively wrapped a beefy arm around my waist. When I didn't back away, he nuzzled my neck gently.

"That's a nice welcome home," he murmured against my skin. I wrapped my arms around his neck and waited until he kissed lightly up my cheek before I turned to kiss him. Nausea rose up in the pit of my stomach as his lips closed over mine and he moaned into my mouth. I fought it back because it would all be over very soon.

"I thought maybe we could do some blow and spend the night fucking," I whispered and ran my hands up his chest to unbutton his work shirt. "I missed you."

"Oh God, Jamie, I missed you, too," he whispered back as he cradled my face in his hands for what I hoped was the very last time. The work shirt hit the floor, and his stomach rumbled.

"I haven't eaten today. Why don't we order some food, do some blow, eat, and then spend the rest of the night in bed?" he asked. I forced myself not to cringe as he played with my hair and waited for me to answer. Once we did the coke, it wouldn't matter anyway, so I agreed. With the decision made, I felt calm when I picked up the phone and ordered a pizza from the local place as he went to take a shower. I sat on the couch to wait and wondered what it would be like to die.

He never noticed the extra powder in the bag as he cut it into lines on the mirror.

I watched with detached interest as line after line reflected in the surface of the glass. He handed me a bill, rolled one for himself, and did the first line. The breath I'd been holding came out in a gush as he grinned and told me to do the next one. So, I closed my eyes, told Brian that I loved him in my head, and tucked the bill into my nose as I inhaled the spiked coke.

The euphoric high rushed through my body like a sweet orgasm as the drugs entered my bloodstream. It took a minute for me to realize that I didn't feel any different from the other times I'd done coke with Steven. My nose burned a little, but I wasn't sick or anything. Maybe I didn't put enough of the rat poison in the coke to make a difference. Steven did another line as I sat back on the couch and watched. Disappointment welled in my chest. I'd thought it was finally going to be over.

Steven coughed, a harsh hacking sound, and I looked up.

"Man, this shit is strong tonight," he commented as he bent down to take the third line. My vision blurred as Steven fell back against the couch with a laugh. Even through the fog of coke, I could tell that his breathing had started to accelerate. Sweat dripped down his flushed face, and he reached for me, and I fell into his arms laughing. The room spun a bit as I straddled him and began to kiss his neck. His hands cupped my ass, and when I closed my eyes, I could smell the sweet scent of coconut. The second line didn't go down as smoothly as the first. In fact, I didn't make it all the way through before I started to feel sick, which made the dizziness worse, so I opened my eyes. Confusion caused me to blink several times as my mind showed me Brian beneath me instead of Steven. His sweet face broke into a smile, and I lost myself in warm brown eyes. Driving him back against the couch with the force of my kiss, I caressed his face with my fingers and felt nothing but Brian's skin.

"I love you so much," I told Brian as his lips met mine again. My lips moved to his neck as he reminded me that he loved me just as much, and that he forgave me. When his hand slid into my loose shorts and cupped my cock, I thrust my hips forward, welcoming the touch. I loved to feel Brian's hands on me. Getting hard under his fingers, my cock throbbed, and I let my back arch as I rubbed myself shamelessly against him. My Brian wouldn't care if I acted like a whore, as long as I only did it with him.

"Up, stand up, baby… I want you in my mouth," Brian said, and after a few tries, I got to my feet on the couch. Straddling his lap, I balanced myself by putting my hands on his shoulders. They felt bigger than normal, but I refused to open my eyes to look. The feeling of his hands on my skin as he pulled my shorts and briefs down felt like pure sin. God, I wanted him. I missed Brian so much. A soft, wet tongue rubbed over the head of my cock and my knees went weak.

"Yeah, God, I love your mouth," I moaned, thrust my hips forward, and felt his sweet mouth surround my dick. Quiet, agonized moans fought their way out of me, while I listened to the erotic sucking sounds he made around my shaft. With a groan, I began to thrust gently into his mouth. A strong hand reached up between my legs and stroked my balls as I entwined my fingers in his hair. It felt different than his normal curls, but I concentrated on the feeling of his mouth instead.

At my needy whimper, he sucked harder and used his other hand to stroke me in time with his lips. I struggled to breathe as he deep throated me and nearly begged him to let me ride his cock. It had been so long, and I needed to feel Brian inside me.

A cell phone rang, distorted in my head, as if it were ringing at the end of a long tunnel. When I opened my eyes and looked down, just on the verge of an explosive orgasm, I saw Steven look up at me. My heart broke when I realized in my drug-induced haze that it hadn't been

Brian. It took me a minute to get my pants up and climb off the couch while Steven's arm flailed out for the phone and managed to grab it on the fourth ring.

"O'Dell," he said, slow and heavy into the phone. "Oh. Yeah, send him up." He hung up and looked at me. "The pizza… pizza guy. Wallet… on the… the counter." His labored breathing made each word come out in a huff. It took me a second, but then I remembered the poison in the coke and felt a momentary joy that we were so close to the end. I took a deep breath and wondered if I should just do another line of coke and forget about the door. In a moment of clarity, I suddenly knew that I didn't want anyone to find us until after—no hospitals, no resuscitation. My Brian was dead, and I didn't want to live without him. No matter what my mother said, I knew that he would be in Heaven because he was better than most of the church people I'd ever met. Kind, generous, and loyal—if anyone deserved to be in Heaven with God, Brian did. I knew I wouldn't be so lucky. Taking Steven's life would earn me a one-way ticket to Hell, but I had no other choice. I couldn't let him hurt anyone else because of me. I'd pay that price.

The room swam as I grabbed Steven's wallet from the breakfast bar. When I walked past the couch to answer the door, I noticed that he had stopped moving. I didn't know if he was still breathing. The air in the apartment had started to solidify, and the door seemed so fucking far away. Brian's face swam before my eyes—not the Brian from California, but the sweet boy that I kissed that day in our tree house.

"I love you," I told him as my knees gave out and the plush gray carpet rushed up to slam into my face.

CHAPTER EIGHT

"SO, WHAT'S his name?"

"Sam, he was my roommate freshman year. This is his senior year, so we moved into an apartment together. It's been amazing."

"That's great. Any plans for after college?"

"Yeah, he wants to go to graduate school out here actually, so I may be applying to... hey, I think he's waking up."

The conversation didn't make any sense to me, and I couldn't make my brain function enough to figure out who the voices belonged to. My head and chest ached, which confused me further. I didn't understand how I could be in pain if I were dead. When my hands flexed involuntarily, I felt a pinch on the top of the right one, so I made an effort to relax it. Sounds were becoming clearer as my mind started to focus on my surroundings. I could hear a sort of rhythmic beeping, something—a cart, maybe—being rolled across the floor, and murmured conversations. The room seemed bright outside of my closed eyes, but I just didn't want to open them yet, afraid of what I might see.

"Jamie, can you hear me?"

The voice sounded so familiar, but the pain in my head wouldn't allow me to concentrate long enough to figure out who spoke. I blinked rapidly against the blinding light of the room. The face in front of me seemed to radiate with an ethereal glow, framed by soft, iridescent brown curls. My breath caught in my throat as he smiled, and I knew in that moment that I was dead.

"Brian," I whispered, the name scratching out of my dry throat through cracked lips. His smile grew, and tears welled in my eyes. I never thought I would see him again, and I wondered again where we were, or maybe if he was a hallucination or a vision sent to torment me.

The vision explanation seemed more and more likely as Brian's face distorted around the edges, as if he were melting. I felt a wave of nausea when the room started to tilt and spin as if I'd been drinking heavily. Fear made adrenaline course through my blood, and as I reached out for Brian, I noticed that my arm trembled. Nothing came out when I tried to talk, just gurgling nonsense.

My body went rigid, as if someone had shoved an iron bar down my spine. I couldn't move; I couldn't even breathe. A helpless tear fell down my cheek seconds before my body started to convulse. I heard Brian scream, and everything faded to a white blur.

WHEN I woke next, all I could feel was a dull, exhausted ache. Everything from my head down to my legs hurt, almost as if I'd been in some kind of accident. Too tired to attempt to understand, I opened my eyes to an empty room. Disappointment flooded my chest, and I squeezed my eyes closed to stop the welling of pain in my heart. Brian must have existed only in my imagination. A choking sob tore from my throat, and I couldn't stop the tears from falling. A toilet flushed somewhere in the distance, and I heard the sound of a door opening.

"You're awake." A pale boy with short blond hair and glasses wiped his hands on his faded jeans and came to stand by my bedside. "I'm Adam. I've heard a lot about you, Jamie." Tired and confused, I just nodded. I really didn't care what he was talking about.

"Where…?" I started to ask when the door to my left opened and Brian walked into the room. A sling held up his right arm. His eyes were shadowed and haunted. Our eyes met, and he turned quickly to sit on the edge of the bed.

"You scared me so badly," he whispered. His left hand hovered a few inches above mine for a moment before he let it fall onto his leg.

"I thought you were dead," I whispered back. I really wanted to reach over and take his hand, but my arms ached. Too tired to move just yet, I stayed still and looked up into his face. The exhaustion I saw framing his red-rimmed eyes, the stubble on his face from days without shaving, and the way he didn't touch my hand all had me worried. I still hadn't accepted that Brian was real, but his distance bothered me all the same. "Where are we?"

"You're in the hospital. They brought you in two days ago, and this is the first time your eyes have been open." His breath caught on the last few words, as if they were hard for him to say. I wanted him to crawl into bed and hold me, as he had when we were at the apartment, but he wouldn't touch me.

"What's wrong with me?" I didn't know what had happened earlier, or if it would happen again, and I didn't like not knowing. Brian hesitated and looked up at the other guy standing next to him.

"What do you remember?" Brian asked, his voice tentative, almost careful. I closed my eyes and tried not to think about it, but the words came anyway.

"I remember watching you get shot in the chest. I remember watching the blood spread across your T-shirt as I tried frantically to get to you. I remember being bashed in the head just after you collapsed. I don't remember too much after that except begging that fucking prick to let me call an ambulance. That's when he told me that it was too late, that you were dead. Then, I died, too, only my body didn't understand that yet. I remember how much I hated myself, how much I hated him. Things get blurry after that, but I do remember finding the rat poison and putting it in the coke, and I sort of remember how peaceful I felt doing the lines and knowing that it was over." The horrified look on Brian's face stopped me cold. I swallowed hard as I realized what I'd just said.

"Adam, I think we need to talk alone for a few minutes. Can you…?" Brian started, but Adam just put his hand on Brian's arm.

"I'm going to go get some food. After being kicked in the head so many times in karate, you know, my short term memory is for shit," he said as he squeezed Brian's shoulder and then headed for the door. "If I don't get a text from you, I'll just head back to the hotel. I'm sure Sam has found something for us to do this afternoon. It was great to see you again." Brian nodded, still shell-shocked, and Adam left the room.

"Who is he?" I asked before Brian could start asking about my confession. It didn't really matter, but I was curious, and it would help me stall for time.

"That's Adam." At my blank look, Brian frowned slightly, and then his voice sounded worried, "Don't you remember? I told you that I started karate after I got out of the hospital back in Alabama. Adam and I met at the dojo and became really good friends. He happened to be here with his boyfriend touring graduate schools when he read my post about you being in the hospital. When he sent me a message, I said he could come and see me here." Brian shrugged and went very quiet and still for a moment before tears began to roll down his sweet face. "Why, Jamie? Why would you…? I don't understand." He took a deep breath, and I waited for him to gather his thoughts before he tried again. "Why would you try to kill yourself? Why didn't you just let him do the stuff and…?"

"I thought you were dead. He told me you were, and I didn't want to stay here without you. Doing the drugs with Steven was only to keep him from hurting anyone else like he hurt you. I just couldn't stand it, knowing that it was all my fault. I hated myself so much. I still do," I admitted and finally looked away from his tear-streaked face.

"God damn it, Jamie," Brian choked, stood up, and walked to the window near my bed. "Just when I think you've stopped, you find a whole new way to break my fucking heart." I actually felt the pain wash over me in a dizzying wave of fear and heartache. The hopeless surrender in his voice made it sound as if he'd given up. Brian had never said anything to me, not once, to make me think he didn't want to be with me anymore, but that sentence hurt me to my very core.

"I thought you were dead," I repeated in a broken whisper. "I just couldn't keep going anymore." He continued to stare out the window, but I could see him shaking. The quiet sob that broke from him was like a knife in my chest, and I tried to roll to my side to get out of bed and go to him. Brian glanced over and came back to sit next to the bed.

"Don't get up, Jamie, please," he told me quietly before sitting back down on the chair next to the bed. The hand not held up by the sling rested in his lap.

"I saw you fall, I thought…. What happened after he… after we left?"

"The doctor said that the bullet went right through my shoulder. If he'd shot me on the left side, or in the stomach or something it would have been worse. My cell phone was on the table near where I fell. I called Mike. He called an ambulance and told them he was my brother so he could get in to be with me," he explained.

"Thank God," I murmured, mostly to myself.

"The hospital called the police and I told them that I didn't know the person that shot me because I was so afraid that he would hurt you if the police cornered him. They came to see me so many times, I was sure they didn't believe me. But then, the pizza guy found you and they got you to the hospital. When they told me that O'Dell was dead, I told them the whole story."

"How did you know I was here?"

"Hartley. He fucking knows everybody, and someone called him when they heard about you and O'Dell."

For several long minutes, neither of us spoke, and the silence between us hung like a wet blanket, heavy and thick. I wanted to tell him that I loved him and ask him why he felt a million miles away.

The hospital room door opened then, and a man I didn't recognize came in. The shirt and tie made me think that maybe he worked at the hospital. Hair covered only about a third of his shining, bald head, and he pushed wire-rimmed glasses back up on his nose as he read from a clipboard of paper in his hands.

"James, my name is Dr. Liskey," he said as he strode to my bed. I looked over at Brian, who turned around to listen. "How are you feeling?"

"I don't know; tired, I guess. My arms and legs are sore." I didn't know exactly what he wanted to know, so I left it at that. What I really wanted was for him to leave so that Brian and I could talk. Scared, confused, and exhausted, I didn't want things to go unsaid with Brian. More than anything, I was worried that he would leave. At some point, my behavior would push him too far, and I needed to know it hadn't come to that. I tried to catch Brian's eye, but he was watching the doctor.

"That's normal after a seizure," the doctor commented and began to flip through the papers on his clipboard. My eyes snapped away from Brian and back to the doctor.

"I had a seizure?"

"Yes, you've had two since you were admitted. We're trying different anticonvulsants to see which will work best. The warfarin in the rat poison has caused a seizure disorder within your brain. The condition is most likely permanent but may be at least partially controlled with medication." He seemed to try to break the news gently, but it still took a minute before I could really breathe again. I tried to speak, but I couldn't think of anything to say. It felt like my brain had gone numb with the shock of it.

"We're going to keep you here for a few days, at least, so we can monitor your progress. We'll medicate you to help with the withdrawal, and I'll be sending a social worker in to talk to you about a rapid detox and rehab program. Drugs will cause serious complications with the seizures and medications you'll be on. You need to stop, or it will kill you." He delivered the stern warning with a gentle hand on my shoulder. "I'll be back in to check on you tomorrow, but if you have any questions, the nurses can contact me." I couldn't reply, so I simply nodded as I stared at the ceiling, unable to process the idea that I would have seizures for the rest of my life.

Brian's heavy, frustrated sigh burned in my ears, and with a huge effort, I rolled to face the wall. Terrified and alone, I found that I was too tired even to cry. I stared at the protective railing on the side of the bed and tried to figure out what the fuck I was going to do. No one would hire me if I fell over having fits all the time. I didn't even think I'd be able to drive anymore.

The bed dipped behind me, and I felt Brian climb in with me. Scooting as close to me as he could to fit in the tiny, cramped space, he slid his arm around my waist and pulled me back against his chest. His arm, still in the sling, pressed into my back. I wanted to take comfort in his arms, but I couldn't, not if he didn't love me anymore. The tears came then, and I didn't try to stop them.

"Jamie, it's going to be okay," Brian whispered against my hair.

"Is Steven dead?" I asked dully, unsure which answer would be better. Maybe if Steven knew I was defective, he'd leave me alone. I couldn't process the idea that I'd taken someone's life, no matter how reprehensible that life was.

"The pizza guy that delivered to your apartment heard you fall on the other side of the door. He got the manager to open up the door for what they called a 'wellness check'. O'Dell was already dead, but you were just barely breathing, so he called an ambulance. The police… well, they think that O'Dell just got a bad batch of coke." Brian knew better, and it disgusted him. Even as upset as I was, I noticed that he hadn't called me "baby" or "honey," his fingers hadn't rubbed against my chest, and he hadn't kissed me once.

"I… I need to know," I started but then faltered. God, I needed to know if he still loved me, but I was so scared of finding out the answer. He moved back a fraction and pulled me so I lay on my back. His expression softened when he looked at me.

"Need to know what?" he asked, letting his hand rest on my chest. He didn't touch my face or my hair, and it killed me inside.

"If you still love me," I whispered. He hesitated and blew out a breath, which I felt against my face. I tried to roll back over so that I couldn't see him when he answered. I couldn't take him looking me in the eye and telling me that he didn't. He held me firmly with the hand on my chest, and I was too tired to try to fight. I stared at the sling on his arm instead.

"I do love you, Jamie...." The unspoken "but" hung heavy in the air, and I waited for my heart to break. I looked up into his face and saw that his eyes were closed, like the pain of what he needed to say had overwhelmed him.

"But you don't want to be with me," I offered. His eyes opened, but his hesitation said everything. I nodded and silently wished that he'd get out of my bed so that I could go to pieces. It only made sense. Everyone else had left me. I was a lying, murdering, piece of shit drug addict whose own parents didn't want him.

"I want to be with you, Jamie, but we need to take time to get shit sorted out first. I don't know how to help you with your addiction. You snuck out of our apartment to buy drugs, and you didn't even talk to me about it. I thought you were handling the withdrawal. God damn it, I'd have given you the fucking money, but you... you...." He buried his face in my neck, and I wrapped my arms around him. "I love you, Jamie, but I just can't trust you right now. The doctors are going to help your body beat the addiction, and then we're going to figure out how to get you into rehab."

"But just as my friend...," I said dully, and he pulled back to look at me.

"As your best friend," he said quietly. "One day, you and I will look back, and we'll talk about what's happened between us. For right now, we're going to look forward, okay?" I nodded and held him when he made no move to get out of bed or out of my arms.

I held onto him as long as I could because I didn't know if I'd ever be able to do so again.

MIKE and Alex came to visit me the next day, relieving Brian to go home, shower, and change. I'd told Brian that he didn't have to stay with me, but the sentiment was halfhearted at best. If I were perfectly honest with myself, the thought of being alone terrified me. I thought maybe if he left one day, he'd never come back, and I would have no one.

I was sitting in a chair next to the bed because the nurses wanted to get me "up and moving," claiming I'd feel better. Alex threw his arms around me and knelt next to the chair. He spoke quietly, as if he were visiting the deathbed of a loved one.

"I missed you so much."

Pulling my feet up into the plush chair, I wrapped my arms around my knees. Over the last few months, I'd lost so much weight that I fit easily. My head drooped, and my aching body felt worn out.

"I missed you, too." The response was automatic, mechanical. Part of me felt that way, but the overwhelming depression made me apathetic. Alex would leave, just like everyone else had, so it didn't make any sense to get attached. The seizures, the drugs, or my appalling behavior would drive him away, and I couldn't stand the thought of another rejection, especially not by Alex. Mike stood over by the window. I didn't look up, but I could feel him watching us.

"How are you, baby?" Alex asked and put his hand on top of mine. That simple gesture, the pet name, all the things that Brian wouldn't do anymore—they hurt so much.

"I'm okay," I mumbled as I stared at the IV taped to my hand and wished they'd leave. The only thing I hated more than being alone was being with people, but I was so scared to be alone.

"Of course you're not. You look like if someone touched you, you'd break into a million pieces," he whispered and pushed a strand of hair back behind my ear. When I looked up and our eyes met, something inside me shattered. Almost imitating the duck-and-cover position we'd learned in school, I grabbed the back of my neck and slammed my forehead into my knees. I wanted to curl up tight enough into a ball that no one could hurt me again. Until Alex put his arms around me and held me still, I hadn't realized that I was rocking in the chair.

"I don't know what to do," I admitted. "The doctor said I'll keep having seizures. I don't know how I'm going to pay for being in the hospital. They want me to go to rehab, but I can't do that. I don't have any money. I don't have anything. I don't even have a place to live once I leave here. Brian doesn't want to be with me anymore. I can't… I can't…." My breathing turned to shallow gasps, as if I were crying but with no tears. Mike came over then and knelt in front of my chair. He took my face in his hands and forced me to look up.

"You have friends, Jamie, lots of them. We are going to help you because that's what family does. Please, just worry about getting better and getting out of here," he said quietly, and I just stared at him, shocked by his words.

"But… but you hate me," I stuttered. I felt my face heating up from unshed tears as he took his hands from my face. The shock must have registered in my expression, because he started to justify his comfort.

"Brian told me why you did what you did. For a long time, I thought you were just jerking him around. I didn't believe, even after Alex tried to tell me, that you really did love him. The fact that you wanted to die rather than live without Brian, that you'd take that fucking bastard with you rather than risk letting him hurt Alex, made me realize that Alex was right. I'm sorry, Jamie. I know we got off to a bad start, but I admit when I'm wrong, and I'd like for us to be friends." Mike smiled when Alex linked their fingers together and then kissed his hand.

"And I've never stopped being your friend, Jamie. I know we didn't get to see much of each other after I moved into the boarding house, but I missed you. I missed our pizza nights with stupid romance movies. I missed sitting around the studio with you and making fun of the other models when they weren't looking. Before Mike, you were the only one who ever wanted me to be myself. How could you think that I'd walk away from you when you need me?" Alex asked, his eyes never leaving mine.

"Thank you," I whispered and hugged myself tighter as I noticed movement coming from the hall. Brian came in through the open door to my hospital room, followed closely by Richard and Carolyn.

"Look who I found wandering around the airport," Brian said as Alex and Mike stood back out of the way. They looked a little sheepish, no doubt remembering their last encounter with Brian's parents. "Thank God they didn't go to the boarding house." Mike, Alex, and Brian all laughed, but Carolyn made her way to my side. I watched as her eyes swept over me and she shook her head.

"You're so thin, sweetheart," she said as Brian pulled over one of the visitor chairs so she could sit next to me. I couldn't stand to wonder what she thought of me—drug addict, whore, and perpetual fuck-up. She probably never wanted me to see Brian again. Instead, she surprised me by taking my hand in hers. She simply sat with me, letting me feel her concern through our joined hands. Richard put a hand on my shoulder and told me he wanted to go find out about my condition since technically he was still my family physician. After he left, the room went silent for a long time. None of us wanted to speak. No one seemed to want to address the elephants in the room: the addiction and the seizures.

After about twenty minutes, Richard returned with a grim expression and sat on the bed.

"Your doctor said he explained about the seizures and about rehab," Richard said solemnly. I just nodded as shame colored my face.

"I think he should come and stay with us," Carolyn said and looked to her husband for confirmation that she did not receive.

"He needs to be in a facility where they can address his needs, Carolyn. I could've helped treat his addiction medically, but he needs support from someone trained in the psychological aspect of addiction. If he doesn't learn to deal with that, the medical part won't be successful," Richard told her, and after a moment, she nodded.

"I can't afford any kind of rehab, Dr. Schreiber, so it doesn't really matter anyway," I told him honestly. "I don't even know how I'm going to pay for the hospital stay."

"Well," Brian said as he rested his hand on his mother's shoulder. "I don't think I told you, but when those guys put me in the hospital back in senior year, it happened inside the school. With the other stuff that had already happened, Dad said they failed to address the problem and sued them. They settled the lawsuit a couple of weeks ago, and after the legal fees and everything, he gave me twenty-five thousand from the settlement. That should at least take care of the rehab."

"No," Richard and I both said together. Brian seemed to know that I'd disagree, but he looked surprised by his father's argument.

"That money is for you to do something with your future. We'll find another way to help Jamie," he told Brian sternly. Brian tried to argue, saying that it was his money and he could do what he wanted, but Richard would not back down. I got the feeling that once Brian had the cash in his possession he would do whatever he wanted with it, no matter what either of us said.

The debate over rehab seemed to break up the party. Mike and Alex had a shoot that afternoon, and Richard wanted to get settled in at the hotel. Mike offered to drop them. After the four of them hugged me and told me they would see me the next day, they left. Brian kicked off his shoes and sat cross-legged on the bed.

"I'm not going to argue with you about this because I'm too fucking tired, but you are not paying for my rehab. I got you shot. I think I've done enough," I said and reached down on the side of the chair to pull the lever that flipped up the footrest. When my feet were resting comfortably, I tugged the blanket higher onto my shoulders and closed my eyes.

"I never blamed you for what happened that day, Jamie."

I kept my eyes closed and wrapped my arms around myself under the thin shelter of the blanket. Maybe if I pretended I'd fallen asleep, we wouldn't have to have this conversation. He'd blame everything on Steven or, worse, blame it on himself.

"If you're tired, why don't you come and lay on the bed?" he said quietly. It sounded like an invitation to lie in bed with him, and I hesitated. If he just wanted to be friends, we didn't need to start blurring those lines. When I opened an eye to look over, I saw that he'd moved from the bed to one of the chairs, and my heart sank. As much as I thought we shouldn't blur the lines, I wanted so badly to feel his arms around me.

My body felt like lead as I pulled myself to my feet and stumbled over to the bed so that I could sleep and not have to think about the nightmare my life had become.

CHAPTER NINE

BRIAN'S head lolled to the side as he half lay in the reclined chair next to my bed. I'd tried at least half a dozen times to get him to go home to sleep, but he wouldn't leave my side. Even though he never mentioned it, I think he knew how much the seizures scared me. He wouldn't leave me to go through them alone. He couldn't let me face anything alone. In fact, earlier, we'd continued the argument from the day before about him using the settlement to pay for rehab. Nothing I said seemed to deter him. With each day that I grew stronger, I came closer to leaving the hospital. I doubted that I could keep refusing him forever.

"He looks just like he did when he was a boy," Carolyn said from the door, nearly giving me heart failure. I'd seen Brian sleeping a lot lately, both when we were together at the apartment and here in the hospital. I loved seeing how relaxed his face looked when all of the stress and worry had left it. Sometimes, he had nightmares, but not always. I'd have given anything to crawl into that chair and wrap myself around him. Aside from the fact that he no longer wanted me to, if I had another seizure, he'd just end up covered in vomit, drool, and piss.

"Hi, Carolyn, Richard isn't with you?" I asked, surprised when she entered the room alone. She glanced at me with a smile and then walked over quietly to push Brian's hair back from his eyes.

"He needs a haircut," she said, the love in her voice unmistakable. It made me miss my own parents with a blinding pain. "Richard had a few errands he needed to run. He'll be along in a while." I wondered what kind of errands he would be running in San Diego, but I didn't say anything. If she'd wanted to tell me, she would have.

"Oh, well, thank you for coming." I hit the button on the television remote that raised the head of the bed. Like a slow-motion corpse rising from the grave, I sat up in bed. Even though I'd just woken from a nap, I still felt tired. Being either in bed or sitting down most of the time had drained me of what little energy I had left. I felt like my life was on the edge of a cliff, and if I moved too much one way or another, it would all be over. Unfortunately, every direction seemed to be the wrong direction.

We sat in awkward silence for nearly an hour, pretending to watch the television that played overhead. The court show where one neighbor sued another over a fallen tree had just changed to yet another talk show when Brian started to stir.

"You don't need a gun...," he mumbled and gripped the blanket in his fists. He shifted in the chair, and his head jerked to the side. "Don't hurt him...."

"Carolyn...," I said, but she was already up and going over to wake him. He jerked when she shook his arm and called his name. With a sharp, deep breath, he blinked rapidly and looked around like he was surprised to find himself in a hospital room recliner and not on the floor at the apartment, bleeding to death.

"Mom?"

"It's okay, honey. It was just a dream," she said softly as she smoothed down the wild side of his hair. He used his heels to flip the footrest of the recliner down and sat up, almost as if he were afraid of falling back to sleep. Brian glanced around the room for a second and then asked her where Richard was. She gave him the same explanation about errands, and I could tell that he didn't buy it either.

A knock on the door surprised us all.

"James, my name is Detective Sanchez, and this is my partner, Detective Isaacs. We'd like to talk to you about what happened in your apartment the other night. Do you feel up to talking to us?" I looked up to see two men in suits standing just inside my hospital room door. Brian sat up straighter in the chair next to my bed and rested the paperback he'd been reading on the arm.

"Jamie, you really should talk to a lawyer," Brian warned. He stood up as the two men entered the room and stood next to my bedside. As the first officer took out a small notebook, Brian took my hand. Of course, I knew he was just trying to comfort me because I was exhausted after the seizure I'd had that morning, but the gesture felt so natural my heart ached.

"And you are?" The second cop asked, looking over at Brian evenly.

"Brian Schreiber, I'm a friend of Jamie's."

"And you?" He asked Carolyn as the first cop noted Brian's name in his notebook.

"Carolyn Schreiber, Brian is my son," she said, and I heard her voice shake, ever so slightly.

"Mr. Schreiber, Mrs. Schreiber, would you mind waiting in the hall so that we could talk to Mr. Mayfield alone?" The request came out more like a statement, and Brian squeezed my hand.

"I'll be okay," I told them gently as I squeezed back. Brian and Carolyn really didn't need to hear all of the gory details of that last night with Steven, though I admit that I didn't want to be alone with the police in my hospital room.

Brian kissed my forehead and then walked slowly toward the open door leading to the hall. He stood back and waited for Carolyn to go first before the first officer, Detective Sanchez, let it close behind them. Once the door clicked, the detective joined his partner at my bedside. I slid up higher in the bed, trying to find some kind of equal footing with them, but failed. Feeling like a little boy, I pulled the blankets up a little higher over the flimsy gown and waited.

"James, can you tell us the nature of your relationship with Steven O'Dell?" Detective Sanchez asked, pen poised with a calm tone and expression.

"He was my manager," I said truthfully, trying not to elaborate.

"Your manager for…?" the second cop asked, and I noticed he didn't have a little notebook. Apparently, the first guy took all of their notes.

"For adult videos."

"People that we've spoken to indicated that your relationship was pretty volatile. Would you say that's true?"

"Yes."

"Can you tell us a little about that?" The second cop had pulled up a chair next to the bed to sit down. I didn't know if the gesture was supposed to make me feel more comfortable with them being there or to lull me into telling them my darkest secrets.

"We argued a lot. He hit me," I told them and knew that my answer probably sounded evasive, but I didn't know what would get me in trouble.

"What kinds of things did you argue about?" He tried again.

"Money, sex, our relationship—the things people usually argue about."

"Yes, but usually when people argue, one of them doesn't end up dead." The second cop pointed out, and I conceded with a nod.

"What happened that night, James?" The first cop asked, pulling up a chair for himself. Now they were my buddies. Everyone was comfy and cozy. I didn't want to talk about that night, especially not with the police. Stalling for time, I tried to look like I was gathering my thoughts. My head ached, and I couldn't decide how much or what to tell them.

It didn't matter because before I could answer, Richard walked in through the door with another man. When I glanced over to see who the second man was, something caught my attention about the familiar way he stood with his arms folded across his chest. His thinning brown hair and lean frame didn't seem familiar at all, just the way he stood. When the man looked up at me, I saw his sapphire blue eyes, the eyes that were just like mine.

"If you have any more questions for my son, you can contact my attorney," my father said, handing Detective Sanchez a business card.

"James is over eighteen, and can talk to us without a lawyer present if he chooses," the second officer said as he stood up from his spot next to the bed. He looked over my father's shoulder at me. "James, would you like to continue to talk to us?"

"I...," I started, but nothing else would come out. The shock of my father standing in the same room, the overwhelming fear, paralyzed me.

"Jamie, tell them no. Talk to your dad first." The calm, rational voice belonged to Brian. He was the one I trusted more than anyone else, including myself. I nodded to him, making sure that the officers saw.

"Can he get your business card and call when he's ready?" Brian asked the second cop, who pulled a business card from his suit pocket. Finally, I found my voice.

"I do want to talk to you. It's just that I've been having seizures and everything is just so jumbled up in my head right now." The justification sounded childish and wrong, but it's all I could think of to get them to leave.

"We'll give you a call tomorrow to see how you're feeling," the first cop hedged, and I nodded. After they'd left the room, my father walked toward me, and I started to climb backward on the bed, terrified of what would happen next.

"No… no, no… I won't go back to that place. I'm an adult now—you can't make me," I cried as panic burned in my throat. Brian strode over to the bed and stood between my father and me with his arms crossed.

"You never told me that you found him!" my father yelled at Brian, who stood firm and tall in the face of his rage. The lines of Brian's back were tense but beautifully strong. I wanted to run my fingers over the taut muscles, just to feel close to him, but I stayed still.

"You never told me that he called you, homeless and begging for help, and you turned him away!" Brian yelled back before letting one of his hands rest on my leg, and I felt comforted by the gesture. My father's face, which just a second before had been red with anger, paled.

"What do you mean?" he asked and looked around Brian to see me. "Jamie, what does he mean?"

"He means that three days after I left the Center, when I was terrified and alone, living on the streets in San Diego, I called your house. Your *wife* answered and told me that I was no longer your son and she didn't care where I went so long as I never came home." My voice shook slightly as I replayed the phone call in my head. Brian turned to look at me. I had never given him the whole truth about that conversation because I didn't want to unleash all the horrors of my time on the streets to him.

"I didn't know," my father said as he retreated a step and his back hit the wall. "She never told me." He covered his eyes with a hand and tried to hide his emotions from the room. After a long moment, he took a breath to steady himself. "I hired investigators, former cops, and street kids, anyone I could find that might help me find you. They searched for six months and found nothing. It killed me not knowing where you were." A tear ran down his cheek, but I refused to let myself feel anything but anger toward him.

"Why? So you and your wife could stick me back in that place? Do you know what it's like to spend a year having people tell you that you're worthless and wrong? Do you know what it's like to be a high school dropout because your parents couldn't stand the sight of you?" I asked, the rage building in my head. Turning toward Brian, I swung my legs over the side of the bed and stood. If I had to face the bastard, I was going to do it on my own two feet.

"I never wanted you to go there, but your mother was so determined," he said and shook his head. "I thought maybe it wouldn't be so bad for you, and then she'd get used to the idea of you being gay. When I came to see you that last time, and I saw the dead look in your eyes, I told her that I wanted you to come home. She argued, but in the end, I told her I would leave and take you with me if she didn't agree. When she relented, I went to the Center to get you, but you were already gone. No one would tell me where you'd gone. I've never been so scared."

Brian looked at me and then reached down to take my hand. No matter what our relationship had turned into, I felt thankful for him then.

"Where is she?" I asked, not sure I wanted to know the answer. The cold sound of her voice still rang in my ears when I was alone in the dark.

"We separated," he admitted. "After I went to the Center and you weren't there, I was frantic. She argued with me when I hired those people to find you. She said it was God's plan, and we should just let you be. I realized then that she cared more about her church than she did about either of us. She packed her stuff and moved to a small room at her church, and I stayed in the house. I couldn't force myself to move in case you came home."

Dumbstruck, I stood at Brian's side and tried to decide if I believed him. Growing up, my dad had never lied to me, and he had never hurt me. Even when my mother found Brian and me in bed together, he never raised a hand to me. However, he also didn't stop my mother when she did. Not once did he try to shield me from her cruelty. In the end, he had secured the transfer that moved us to San Diego, away from Brian, and put me in the Center.

"I don't know what to do," I whispered to Brian, who let go of my hand and wrapped his good arm around me, pulling my head onto his shoulder.

"You could have warned him, Dad," Brian said to Richard, clearly angry that his father had ambushed me.

"You could have told Mitch that you'd found his son," Richard countered. "If I lost contact with you and didn't know if you were even alive, it would kill me. I went to talk to Mitch about helping Jamie. I thought maybe if I talked to him as one father to another, I could convince him to help. It surprised me when I didn't have to convince him at all. From the conversation we had when Jamie overdosed and you refused to take him to a hospital, I thought that Jamie might be in danger from him. You never mentioned that you'd talked to him and knew he was looking for Jamie."

"You knew he was searching for me?" I asked quietly. It wasn't that I thought Brian would ever try to hurt me, but the news that he hadn't told me my father wanted to see me surprised me. Brian turned his head and kissed my forehead.

"I tried to tell you, but you said you never ever wanted me to talk about your parents. Then you told me about calling them, and I thought your father lied to me. I thought maybe he wanted to trick me into telling him where you were so he could put you back in that place," Brian admitted.

"I didn't lie to you," my father said quietly, and it sounded as if all of the fight had gone out of him. "Jamie, I love you more than anything else on this earth. I don't want you to worry about anything. I'll take care of the hospital and rehab. Richard said that the doctor is going to discharge you tomorrow. You can come and stay with me for a while until you decide what you want to do."

"You don't even know me."

"I've known you all your life. I know that I've missed the last couple of years, son, but I want to meet the man you've become." My father took a step forward and held out his hand.

"Do you even know why I'm in here?" I asked, unable to keep the sarcasm and skepticism from my voice. As soon as he found out just what he'd missed in the last two years, he'd pull that offer of help right off the table. He nodded first but then seemed to realize that he needed to make me understand.

"You did some bad drugs, which almost… almost killed you and left you with permanent seizures," he said, and remorse showed clearly in his face.

"Yes, thanks to my little forced vacation, your straight-A student turned into a high school dropout, a drug addict, and a porn star. Is that better or worse than being gay?" I knew that it was an unfair question, but I'd wanted to know the answer for years. The little color left drained from his face, and it looked like the wall was holding him upright.

"Oh, Jamie." My name sounded like a gurgle forced past his lips. "Oh, God… I am so sorry. I… I should have stopped her." He pushed away from the wall, and before I knew what had happened, his arms were around me and Brian had been knocked aside. "It's going to be okay now, son, I promise you." I couldn't deny that his comfort and his promises were like redemption for me. Part of me wanted to throw him off, to punish him for what my mother did, but I couldn't. I'd been so scared, wondering what was going to happen to me, that his offer made me feel almost safe.

"What do you think?" I asked Brian as I stepped back from my father's embrace. Over the last two years, I'd made nothing but bad decisions, and I didn't want to make another one because I felt emotional and desperate.

"Your relationship with Brian is okay with me, Jamie. He'd be welcome at our house," my father interjected. My hand trembled just a little as I answered him.

"Brian and I aren't... aren't in a relationship anymore. We're just friends," I told him and noticed Richard and Carolyn glance at each other. Then I looked back at Brian.

"I think that you should stay with your dad when you're discharged tomorrow. He has the money and the resources to find you a top-notch rehab, and he obviously loves you," Brian said softly before reaching up to touch my cheek. The fact that he didn't even try to talk me into staying with him hurt me deeply. I couldn't blame him for wanting the break, but I at least wanted him to make the goddamned offer.

I nodded because I didn't think I'd be able to speak my thoughts without hurting him.

"I think it's time for us to head back to the hotel," Richard told Carolyn with a pointed look. She agreed, picked up her handbag, and went to stand by her husband.

"You guys want to get some dinner?" Brian asked. He kissed my cheek and went over to the other side of the bed to grab his shoes. My gaze drifted to my father and then back to Brian. I didn't want him to leave me alone with my dad. After two years, we really didn't have anything in common anymore. We could talk about me moving in with him, but I just wasn't quite ready to say yes, yet.

Brian hugged me tight before they left and told me that he would be back in a little while. Knowing that he'd be back before I went to sleep made me feel better, and I thought maybe I could face a talk with my father. When we were alone, I lay back down on the bed, suddenly tired from all of the afternoon's stress and activity. He drew up a chair and sat next to the bed with his hand resting on the mattress.

"I know that you don't trust me, Jamie, and I don't blame you. I've given you no reason to. But, I do want you to come and stay with me, even if it's just until you're out of rehab and back on your feet." His voice sounded earnest and emotional.

"Brian thinks I should stay with you, so I will. Apparently, lately, I'm not very good at making decisions for myself, but I trust him," I said, voicing my agreement for the first time. His body relaxed as if someone had let air out of him, and he smiled.

"I'm so glad. We can stop and pick up your stuff on the way home tomorrow, and then we can go to the house, and you can see what else you might like for your room. Everything is still there, but I'm sure you've outgrown some of the stuff you used to like in high school," he said with a quiet laugh. I tried to remember some of the things I did like back then and found that I couldn't. It seemed like a lifetime ago, like that junk belonged to a completely different person.

"Dad, I don't have anything to pick up, and I don't really need anything anyway." My gaze drifted toward the window, and I felt embarrassed to admit that I was essentially homeless, without even a set of clothes to change into when I left. I was sure someone had cleaned out Steven's apartment and sent everything to his brother. The few pieces of clothing that I'd accumulated at the apartment with Brian were things I'd borrowed.

"Jamie, I owe you two years of Christmas presents, birthday presents, and just general spoiling. We are going to get you set up in your new room, buy you some clothes, and figure out where to go from there, and we're going to do it together," he promised and squeezed my hand where it lay on the bed. Wary, I thought it all sounded too good to be true. He didn't need to waste his money on me.

We talked for nearly two hours while Brian went to dinner with his parents. By eight o'clock, I figured he was stalling to give me more time with my dad. When the announcement came over the speakers that visiting hours were over, Brian jogged back into the room.

"Sorry, we stopped at home first, so I could shower and change before dinner. It took longer than I thought it would," he said as he took off his shoes at the door and padded in his socks over to the recliner where he generally slept. He picked up the blanket that had landed on the floor, folded it, and laid it across the chair.

"I should probably get going," my father said and grabbed the hospital pen and note pad that sat near the phone. He wrote down his phone number in big block print. "I'll get things ready for you tonight and be back tomorrow morning. I don't know if they will actually release you tomorrow, but I want to spend more time with you. Is that okay?"

"I'd like that," I said, and deep down, I really meant it because I couldn't deny that I wanted my father back in my life. He should be the one person who always loves me, no matter what else happened. I knew that Brian loved me, but the way he had cut off his affection just killed me.

My father left a few minutes later, and an awkward silence erupted between Brian and me. He stood by the window, which was about as far as he could get from me and still be in the room. I hated the distance between us, both emotional and physical, but I could understand why he wanted to protect himself. I'd been a fucking bastard, and I was lucky he wanted to have anything to do with me at all. After grabbing the remote, which had fallen between the mattress and bedrail, I turned off the television.

"Are you angry with me for telling you that you should stay with your dad?" he asked, but his voice sounded hesitant and almost afraid of the answer. He still hadn't moved from his spot near the window, and I didn't have the strength to ask him to sit next to me on the bed because I was afraid that he would refuse.

"I'm not angry." My voice sounded petulant, like a child who didn't get the ice cream that she wanted. I just needed to stomp my foot and I'd turn into a six-year-old girl.

"But you're upset," he observed. I looked away because I didn't want him to see just how upset. A nurse passed by the door and peeked in before pushing her computer cart further down the hall. I put the call light on, and Brian came over to the bed.

"Are you okay?" He put his hand on my clammy forehead, but I shook him off. The nurse came in and turned off the call light. I liked the nurse on the evening shift—she was a matronly woman with short brown hair, and she always smiled. Even though she had to know why I'd ended up in the hospital, she never looked down on me for it.

"James, is there something you need?" she asked as she checked my machines to make sure everything looked okay.

"Could I get some juice?"

"Sure, honey, we have some on the floor. Would you like apple, orange, or white grape?" she asked me, and her smile couldn't have been warmer.

"Grape, if you have it, or orange, thank you," I said and fell back against the pillow.

"Are you tired? Have you been having any tremors in your arms or legs today?" She checked the little wire taped to my finger, which she'd told me a few days earlier checked my pulse. Then she took my blood pressure with the portable cuff from the corner of the room.

"I am tired, and my hands shook a little earlier, but nothing... I don't know... spastic," I explained. Richard had told me the day before that sometimes my body would jerk for no reason at all because of the damage done to the part of my brain that controls motor function. I'd sat up in bed with a rolling table to eat and accidentally knocked my milk to the floor in an uncontrolled movement of my arm. That moment showed me, more than anything else, that my life would never be normal again.

She brought me the grape juice, and I opened it while she fussed with the sheet on my bed to straighten it. Brian stood by patiently and waited so that we could finish our conversation once she left the room. He rolled his eyes when she went to refill my water pitcher from the sink in the bathroom and asked one final time if I needed anything else.

"I'm fine; thank you," I said, and she smiled before turning to leave. As the door slowly closed, Brian sat down on the bed next to me.

"I don't want you to be upset. I said that I thought it was a good idea because he can take care of you better than I can. He has more money and a nice house. I also think it's a good idea for you to spend some time with him and try to repair some of the damage to your relationship." I nodded and noticed that he didn't mention anything about trying to repair the damage to our relationship.

"I told him that I'd stay with him because I don't have any other options," I said, taking another long drink of the juice. It gave me something to do with my hands and something to focus on besides the desperation I felt from my crumbling relationship. In the back of my mind, I could see myself begging Brian not to leave me, but the logical part of me knew that he had every right. I'd pushed him too far once too often and had to pay the price for my mistakes.

"I'm glad you told him that you'd stay with him, but you do have other options. Leo would have let you stay at the boarding house with us."

My eyes snapped up to his.

"You're not at the apartment?" I asked, and he looked down at the sheet. His face colored slightly, and I reached over to tilt his chin up so I could see his eyes.

"I couldn't stay there, not after the shooting. The blood on the floor reminded me of my parents, and I didn't even get through one night before I called Mike and begged him to come and get me. The landlord was really good about it and didn't even take the cost of cleaning the carpet out of my deposit. I was able to break the lease and move back into the boarding house. Andy and Pete graduated in the spring, and they'd already been looking for a place. I moved in to Andy's old room," he explained. It hurt to think of Brian alone and scared in the apartment after what happened. He'd already had nightmares most of his life, and I hated myself for making them worse. I didn't want either of us to hurt anymore.

"Will you lay with me for a while?" I asked in a whisper. He nodded, stood up, and unbuttoned his jeans awkwardly after taking his arm out of the sling. Once the jeans were on the floor, he slid his arm back into the sling and walked around to the other side of the bed. He relaxed back against the pillow and opened his good arm to me. I rolled over to lay right up against him with my face buried in his neck.

We didn't move again until the nurse came in at midnight to check my stuff and give me my pills. Brian never woke while the nurse worked, and I caught a sweet smile on her face when I kissed Brian's forehead. I loved him so much, and the thought of just being his friend for the rest of our lives tormented me. It wasn't right to hope because he deserved so much better, but I couldn't help it.

One day, I wanted to be worthy of his love again.

CHAPTER TEN

"JAMIE, I'm going to go pull the car around. I'll meet you out front," Dad said as he grabbed my bag and headed for the door. I appreciated him for being sensitive to the need that Brian and I had to be alone for a minute before we went into our uncertain future. The quiet click of the hospital door was the only sound in the awkward silence. Brian stood near the window, which had become his preferred place to be in the small hospital room. The haunted expression on his face as he stared into the distance through the rain-streaked panes of glass tore at me, but I stayed quiet, unwilling to hasten our parting.

The orderly would be there soon to take me down to my father's waiting car. Not wanting the moment to be wasted, I stood up from the recliner chair where I'd sat to put on my shoes. He turned, and the tears in his eyes startled me. With three large, purposeful steps, he was there, and he wrapped a warm hand around the back of my neck. One tear fell as he pulled my face to his. The kiss, full of sorrow and love, lasted just long enough for my heart to break before he put his lips to my ear.

"I love you," he said softly. While I listened to the words carefully, what I heard in them was "goodbye".

He left without another word.

My tears were dry by the time the orderly brought the wheelchair that would take me to my new life. As he wheeled me through the winding corridors, I kept my eyes down and just waited for the ride to be over. When we reached the front doors, I saw my father standing next to a white Lexus sedan with the door open as he waited for me to arrive. His expression remained hopeful and patient while the orderly transferred me to the front seat.

"Ready to go home?" he asked after getting behind the wheel. As much as I wanted to tell him that my home was a tiny studio apartment with Brian, I nodded. I'd allow myself to grieve that night, but then I would focus on the chance my father had given me. I'd let him help me with rehab and maybe some kind of future because after the hell I'd been through in the last two years, I deserved it, even if it couldn't happen with Brian.

When we reached the upscale home that I barely remembered, I told my father that I wanted to lie down for a while just to get out of his eternally optimistic company. Aside from the placement of the windows and the different color paint on the walls, the room at the San Diego house looked a lot like my old room had in Alabama. I stood in the doorway when the wave of nostalgia hit. Brian seemed to be everywhere in the room. If I could just put that inflatable mattress down on the floor, he could stay the night just as he had back home. But we weren't back home, and Brian didn't want to stay the night. He had a new home, with new friends and a new life.

I sat on the bed for a while and just looked around at all the little things I'd forgotten about myself in the last two years. My baseball trophies sat on a shelf over the dresser. A notebook with half-doodled pictures of Brian lay on top of the desk. A list of colleges Brian and I had planned to apply to was pinned to the corkboard above the desk. Even the band posters remained hanging on the walls as a reminder of what my life had been like before my mother decided to ruin it by taking me to the Center.

Stir-crazy and a little depressed, I decided to go through the clothes in my closet to see what fit and what I wanted to keep. Staying busy and wearing myself out might help on my first night back in the house. Pulling out hanger after hanger, I kept most of the jeans, though they were too big. I kept a lot of the T-shirts that I still liked. I tossed my Sunday clothes because I no longer had a need for them. As I started to go through the dresser, I decided to let my father take me shopping for a few things that I wanted. It would make him happy, which I discovered, at least right then, was important to me.

I'd just spotted my favorite tennis shoes at the bottom of my closet when the room lurched and its contents seemed to melt before my eyes. For a minute, I panicked as the pre-seizure symptoms hit me without warning. My legs trembled, and I tried to call for my dad, but I couldn't make anything work. Losing control of my entire body was truly the most terrifying experience I'd ever had, and the worst part was it could just continue to happen at any time. My head hit the desk as I fell, and I tasted blood as the hard wooden edge busted my lip. I managed to land on my side as the nice nurse at the hospital had instructed. Vomit pooled on the hardwood floor in front of my face, and the smell made the nausea worse.

A scream tore through the room just as the seizure took over.

"JAMIE, honey, it's okay. I'm right here." The voice seemed unfamiliar at first, until I opened my eyes and saw my father as he knelt next to me and stroked my hair. The pillow he'd put under my head reeked of regurgitated Chinese food, and I tried to sit up to get away from the smell before it made me sick again.

"Take it slow," he said and tossed the pillow, which landed in the hall.

"Thank you," I murmured, and my voice sounded like I'd swallowed shards of broken glass. I tried to stand, but my tired and sore muscles just wouldn't support me. The exhaustion felt almost like a next-day hangover, only I didn't get the peace of being drunk first.

"Let's get you to the bathroom," my father said as he put one of my arms around his shoulders and helped me stand. Ashamed of the vomit on my face and my piss-soaked jeans, I closed my eyes and felt a tear slide down my face. After a dozen slow, agonizing steps, I stood propped against the sink while my father helped me get undressed. At nineteen years old, I was mortified to need his help. He threw my soiled clothes onto the floor and handed me one warm washrag after another to wash my face and body so that I felt almost human by the time he helped me dress in cartoon pajama bottoms that I had forgotten even existed.

Shedding my remaining scraps of dignity, I crawled into the captain's bed I'd slept in since I was a child. For a moment, I wished that I could bury my face in the pillow and smell coconuts as I had at the apartment. Closing my eyes, I tried to imagine Brian lying next to me in our big bed. He used to be less than an arm's length from me, but he wasn't there. I curled up into a ball under the covers as my heart ached for him.

"WE NEED to meet with the administrator at the clinic at two; let's stop for lunch on the way." Dad's voice had a forced casualness that I hated. It sounded as if he were taking me golfing rather than to be knocked out and treated for opiate addiction. I'm not sure what I expected, maybe for him to be disappointed in me for the drugs or yell at me, but certainly not to be a buddy. It left me off balance, though I had to admit that nothing in my life was too balanced right then.

"Sure, Dad, whatever you want," I said as I stared out my new bedroom window overlooking the perfectly landscaped back yard. It didn't look anything like the fun, kid-friendly yard we had in Alabama. There were no worn spots in the grass caused by boys' spontaneous baseball games. There were no bikes thrown casually up against the fence, and of course, there was no tree house in the tall oak near the garage. I was sure I'd get used to the view, no matter how much it differed from the one I remembered. It hurt to think that I'd be here, away from Brian, long enough for it to feel familiar.

"It's eleven now, why don't you jump in the shower and we can leave by noon," he said as he side-stepped any meaningful conversation that we should have about going to the detox clinic. I didn't know if I wanted to talk about it, but I guess I wanted him to ask. Jesus, I sounded like a teenage fucking girl.

"Can you hang out in here while I take a shower, just in case I... have problems?" Having to ask that question humiliated me, but the thought of having a seizure in the shower scared me. At the hospital, the shower was open, and a nurse stayed to help me.

"I'd planned to, son," he said quietly and put a hand on my shoulder. Looking up at him, I saw the warm smile and felt a little better. As I was growing up, Dad had worked a lot to build his career, and we were never particularly close. Though I didn't want to hope, I thought maybe since it was just the two of us, we could deepen that bond. But there were so many things he didn't know. Any one of them could push him away again. He would leave me, and then I'd be completely alone. I didn't want to think about that, so I got up off the bed, grabbed my clothes, and headed for the shower.

The hot water felt good as I stood under the spray, so I closed my eyes and let it saturate my hair. It had grown out since Steven chopped it all those months before. The curls at the end were even starting to come back and hung in my face sometimes, but I didn't want to cut them off. Brian loved my hair long, and even though things were strained right then, I refused to give up the hope that one day he and I could be together again.

After I got cleaned up, thankfully without any seizures, I dried off and dressed with the door mostly closed. It bugged me that I couldn't lock the door, but I just couldn't afford privacy in exchange for safety. If I had a problem, my dad needed to be able to get in quickly. One more sacrifice in my life I would have to make. I guess that meant no more jacking off in the shower.

"Dad, where is the rehab place?" I asked as he drove us to the restaurant. As he pulled onto the highway, it occurred to me that having uncontrolled seizures meant that I'd never be able to drive again. The realization made my stomach hurt, but I tried not to think about it too much. At that point in my life, each day was just one more small step toward where I needed to go. Right then, I had to get clean. I'd worry about the rest later.

"It's about fifteen minutes from the house if traffic isn't bad," Dad said brightly. I didn't know if his cheerfulness was a front to hide how he really felt, or if he truly enjoyed taking his son to rehab. Since the rehab place ended up being so close to the house, hopefully that meant Dad would be able to take me and pick me up. I didn't want to take a cab.

"In the mood for Mexican?" Dad asked, and I agreed. It didn't matter where we went for lunch. I wanted today to be over. When he came into my room the night before and told me about the appointment, I thought it would be for the actual detox, but it was just a meeting to make sure that facility would be the right one. I didn't understand what difference it made. Didn't they all do the same thing?

The enchiladas ended up being some of the best I'd ever had. The light, comfortable atmosphere in the restaurant relaxed me. Nothing would happen at the rehab place, and the hospital had prescribed enough meds for a few days, so I had nothing to be afraid of. However, the anxious feeling in my stomach refused to go away.

WHEN we pulled into the parking lot of an office building, I thought maybe we were in the wrong place. It didn't look like what I thought a rehab center would be. Though unsure exactly why, I thought it would look like some kind of detention center, with bars on the windows and barbed wire fences. The fact that it looked like a doctor's office surprised me. The building had several floors, and I wondered if they all belonged to the rehab center. Dad parked the car in the adjoining lot, and we walked up to the door together. I trailed just a bit, intimidated by the imposing building, but not so much that I looked reluctant.

An attractive guy in a dress shirt and tie sat behind a desk in the reception area. I got a little lost in his vibrant green eyes as he asked if he could help us.

"We have an appointment with Dr. Lindman," my father informed him, and he asked us to sit in the plush oversized chairs that littered the large, handsome waiting area. The décor included a muted, earthy color scheme that felt almost calming, scenic landscapes, and oceanic murals. I didn't have a lot of time to look around because almost as soon as we sat down, a thin, academic-looking man had appeared from the door behind the reception desk.

"Mr. Mayfield?" he asked, and I assumed he was speaking to my father, so I just stood meekly off to the side. Dad shook hands with the man, who continued to watch me out of the corner of his eye. I wondered if working with addicts had made him wary or if he was naturally guarded.

"Dr. Lindman, thank you for seeing us on such short notice. This is my son, Jamie." The good doctor held his hand out for me to shake, so I did. The longer we stood around making small talk, the more my anxiety grew. I wanted to know what the hell would happen—if these people could even help me.

"It's nice to meet you, Jamie," Dr. Lindman told me, and I couldn't completely repress a sardonic chuckle.

"Dr. Lindman, I wish I could say the same, but under the circumstances...," I replied, and he laughed. My father put his hand on my shoulder, and when I looked up at him, he smiled. My father's closeness relaxed me.

"Why don't we go into my office and talk." Dr. Lindman led the way around the receptionist's desk, and I caught the guy's eye as I passed. He winked, and my face flamed because he really was cute. After walking down a short hallway, we reached a large, open office with floor-to-ceiling windows on the far wall. Impressive-looking, framed certificates covered the space between two sizable bookcases full of mismatched books with titles like *Uncovering the Inner Addict* and *Addicted to Addiction*. The doctor gestured to a black leather couch in front of the bookcases while he took a single wingback chair across from it. My father and I sat side by side on the couch, and I felt like a kid sent to the principal's office.

"Jamie, based on the conversation I've had with your physician at the hospital and your current medical condition, I've drawn up a tentative treatment plan. I'd like to discuss different options with you and your father so that we can proceed," Dr. Lindman explained, and I simply nodded. I had no idea what kind of treatment plan he had in mind, but it sounded like he'd already decided that I'd receive that treatment at his clinic.

"From what I understand, Jamie would undergo a rapid detoxification during which he would be anesthetized and the drugs removed from his system. After that, he would need six to eight weeks of intensive counseling, followed by continued meetings, counseling, and support," Dad confirmed. I glanced sideways at him, touched that he'd done so much research about what I would need in such a short period. He seemed to be deeply committed to my recovery, and that made my heart a bit lighter.

"That's correct. The detoxification takes anywhere from four to six hours depending on the degree of addiction and the amount of drugs currently in his system. It's been nearly a week since he's had street drugs, so the process may be a bit easier on his body, but we need to keep his blood pressure, temperature, and other vitals stable during the process. Once the procedure is complete, we can move him into his room and monitor his progress. When he comes in for the procedure, he'll just need to bring clothes and toiletries for his stay. I'll give you a... Jamie, are you okay?" Dr. Lindman's expression had gone from confident to puzzled as my mouth opened and closed rapidly and I put my hand on my father's arm.

"Dad, I can't stay here, I can't live here. I need to go home with you... Dad, please." My voice had risen to almost a scream in my panic. He was going to leave me here, just like Mom left me at the Sunshine Center. I'd be at their mercy, having seizures, terrified.

"Dr. Lindman, I'm sure you saw in his file that he has seizures. I'm not sure that an inpatient program is appropriate for Jamie." My father's voice wavered, like he wasn't positive he'd made the right decision.

"I can't stay here," I yelled and jumped off the couch, which pushed it back several inches. "Daddy, please." I begged my father as my arms wrapped around my stomach, and I backed away from them until I hit the wall near the door. My heart thudded so hard in my chest, I could nearly feel it in my temples. If I turned just a bit to my left, I could run, but I froze.

"Could you excuse us for a moment?" My father asked as he hurried to my side. He waited until the doctor left to kneel down next to me. "Jamie, what is it?"

"I can't stay here," I whispered.

"I don't want you to stay here. I'd planned to talk to him about an outpatient program because of your seizures. You need to be home with me. But you look terrified, son. What's wrong?" He continued to stay on one knee by my side. With his admission, my heart rate slowed and I took a deep breath to try to calm myself. My hand shook as I wiped it across my mouth, which had suddenly gone very dry.

"You… you're all I have. I'm so scared all the time that you're going to hear something or see something and leave me again. I mean, you couldn't even look at me before Mom took me to the Sunshine Center. You could put me in this place and never come back." Tears welled in my eyes, but I refused to let them fall. Somewhere deep in my mind, I recognized my own overreaction but could do nothing to stop it.

"Jamie, we can talk about what happened before when we get home, but even if you stayed here to get better, I wouldn't leave you. I am so happy to have you back in my life," my father told me and then wrapped his arms around my shoulders. "I love you, more than anything in the world. Nothing that you tell me—about your past, about rehab, or about who you want to be—is going to make me turn away from you. Now, come back and sit on the couch with me, and we can tell Dr. Personality that you're going to be an outpatient." I giggled a little at his nickname for Dr. Lindman and took my father's hand when he offered it to help me off the floor.

"I'm sorry, Dad." I felt like an idiot for freaking out the way I did, but the thought of being alone scared me. It felt like I had no one left, no one but him.

"No need to be sorry, son," he assured me and left me on the couch to get the good doctor. I didn't pay much attention as they worked out the details of my rehab, but I did get the important bits. The detoxification would happen tomorrow, and then my dad would drop me off at the clinic on his lunch break for the daily sessions and pick me up after work. The nurses at the clinic were equipped to handle my seizures, and I'd have an implant of medication to help me not want the drugs. Finding out that I could handle their program was a relief. My fear of the unknown was usually worse than whatever actually happened.

Once my father signed the paperwork and left them a check, we were free to go. Dr. Lindman made sure to remind us that we needed to be back the next morning by 7:00 a.m. to start the prep for detox.

DINNER was a subdued affair as we danced around talk of the procedure. We'd ordered out for pizza because neither of us felt like cooking. As we sat in the living room with our feet up on a highly polished coffee table, the conversation seemed stunted and awkward.

Eventually, we gave up and Dad turned on the baseball game. I'd never been much into sports, but the Padres had apparently gotten into the playoffs, and it took the pressure off us to talk. Dad woke me up during the seventh-inning stretch and told me to go bed.

By three in the morning, I knew I'd never fall back to sleep. The shadows played across the ceiling as I stared at it and waited for dawn to come. I'd never gone under anesthesia for any reason before, and it made me anxious. It didn't occur to me to ask Dr. Lindman what would happen if I had a seizure during the procedure. So many unanswered questions chased each other through my head that sleep eluded me. Finally, around six, my father came in to wake me.

The constant anxiety frayed my nerves as I pulled on the sweats I needed to wear to the clinic. The instructions Dr. Lindman had given me specifically asked that I wear loose, comfortable clothes even though I'd be changing into a hospital gown for the sedation. When I got downstairs, I saw that my father had already eaten and cleaned up the kitchen. Because of the anesthesia, I had to fast. He'd also packed up his tablet PC, a book, and a newspaper so that he would have something to do in the hours that he waited.

"Are you ready for this, Jamie?" he asked as we sat side by side on the couch to put on our shoes. The running shoes he put on were such a stark contrast to the dress shoes he had worn to work my entire life. Many things had changed about my father in the last few years. His relaxed personality was certainly one of them.

"Ready as I'll ever be." My voice was dull but determined as we headed out to the car. It seemed to take less time to get to the rehab center than it had the day before, probably because I dreaded it. When we got up to the door, we rang the bell as Dr. Lindman had asked, and we waited for someone to let us in. It took several minutes, but eventually a slender woman in scrubs opened the door and led us to Dr. Lindman's office.

"Jamie, how are you feeling?" the doctor asked, and I shrugged.

"I'm scared, nauseated, and just really want to get this over with," I replied truthfully. Dr. Lindman said he could certainly understand that feeling but assured me that the detoxification was the safest way to allow the body to rid itself of the poison naturally. The doctor led me into a small room down the hall and left me with a hospital gown and non-skid socks so I could change. My dad stayed with me because, right then, I didn't want to be alone.

"It's going to be okay, Jamie. I'm not going to leave the building, so I'll be right there when you wake up." Dad said, punctuating the sentiment by meeting my eye and nodding. I tried to smile but couldn't quite manage it. "Did you call Brian and let him know what was happening?"

"Thanks, I'll be alright. No, I didn't call Brian. If he wanted to know what was happening with me, he'd have called," I replied, unable to keep the bitterness out of my voice. "He wouldn't have walked out of my life."

"I don't know what happened between you, but it didn't look to me like he walked out of your life. Maybe he just needs a little time."

Shrugging out of my shirt, I set it on top of my discarded shoes, and my dad turned around while I stripped off the rest of my clothes. The gown hung off me like a shroud, and even without a mirror in the room, I could tell how much weight I'd lost. I pulled on the socks and sat down on the paper-covered table to wait. A few minutes passed before one of the nurses came in to put in an IV. It didn't hurt as much as I thought it would. I'd had one in the hospital, too, but they put it in while I was out.

When she left, my dad sat in the room's only chair and looked up at where I sat on the table.

"God, you're so thin," he remarked, and his eyes filled with sadness and regret. On one hand, I felt guilty for worrying him, but deep down I liked that he showed how much he cared so easily. It made the idea that he wanted me for a son easier to believe.

"I'm sure I'll put some weight back on living with you," I told him and crossed my ankles, letting my legs swing back and forth. Nervous energy coursed through me as I waited for them to come, for something to happen.

"You mean because I'm such a wonderful cook?" he asked with a smirk. Back in Alabama, when we were still a family, my mom did every bit of the cooking. It would surprise me if my father could even boil water. With her there, we'd never had to worry about things like cooking or laundry. She took care of the house.

"Because no one will be beating the shit out of me and feeding me drugs," I said, not thinking, as I rubbed the back of my neck. The shocked sound that came from him then made me feel awful. I hadn't really meant to say that out loud, but my nerves were at their limit. I wanted the procedure to be over so I didn't have to be scared of it anymore.

"Brian hit you?"

"No, Dad, of course not. I'm sorry. I didn't mean to say that. I'm just freaking out," I said quickly, but he continued to look at me. "Do you really want to talk about this now?"

"I guess we don't have to, but I want to talk about it sometime." He still looked troubled, and I blew out a heavy sigh as I hopped off the table. I turned around to show him the scars on my back through the untied gown. Turning back to face him, I pulled the material to the side to show him my stomach.

"After I'd been homeless for almost two months, I met a guy who offered me food and a place to stay. He was nice at first, but after a while, he became… well, not so nice. I don't want to get into the whole story here, but Brian and his friends rescued me from him."

"The guy that did that to you, was he the one they found dead when they brought you to the hospital?" Already pale, his face continued to look troubled as his brow furrowed.

"Yes." I certainly didn't want to elaborate on that situation right then.

"Good," my father barked, sounding vindictive. When I glanced at his face, the ferocity in it surprised me. Dad usually had a very even temper, and I don't think I'd ever seen anything rile him. Before I could ask him about it, the door opened. Dr. Lindman came in with two nurses and a man in scrubs. Dad moved back out of the way as they rolled in a gurney.

"Jamie, why don't you hop up on here and we'll move to the procedure room," the unknown man told me, and I looked quickly at my father, who nodded.

"I'll be right there when you wake up," he assured me. I held the gown closed behind me so I didn't give anyone a show as I sat down on the side of the rolling bed. They waited until I'd reclined against the raised side of the gurney and pulled my feet up before covering me with a thin blanket. My breathing became shallower, and I grabbed the rails of the bed on either side of me just for something to hold on to.

"Jamie, son, you're just going to go to sleep. There's nothing to be scared of," Dad said as he put his hand on my arm. "Stress can trigger a seizure; you need to calm down."

"Don't worry, Mr. Mayfield," the nurse to my right said as she attached what looked like part of a syringe to my IV. As she depressed the plunger, she continued, "I've just given him something to relax him." It took a minute, but my body began to feel heavy and slow. It should have panicked me because that feeling indicated the procedure had started. Instead, I just felt mellow, like when I'd smoked some good weed with Steven. As my eyes started to close and darkness enveloped me, I wondered if I'd ever get Steven O'Dell out of my head.

WHEN I woke, the room blazed with light, which confused me. I didn't know if I'd overslept or who I would wake up next to. Someone kept asking for James, and it took a minute for me to realize she was trying to get my attention. Nausea caused a wretched acidic feeling in the back of my throat, and I took several long, deep breaths to keep myself from vomiting. Sound from the room came to me through a thick blanket as the room spun. I blinked a few times and tried to focus on the face in front of me. After several long minutes, shoulder-length blonde hair came into focus and then a woman's smile.

"Hi, James. How are you feeling?" The woman scribbled something on a clipboard as she continued to try to engage me. I turned my head so that she could see that I heard her, but my voice stuck in my aching throat like cotton, and my mouth was bone dry.

"O-Okay...," I managed after swallowing a few times.

"Are you nauseated?"

"Yeah, and my mouth is really dry." I tried to lift my head, but it felt so heavy.

"Those are both normal after anesthesia. We'll get you some ice chips once you're fully awake. We want to monitor you for a couple of hours, and then I'm sure Dr. Lindman will let you go home." Instead of the contempt I expected to find in her face because of my addiction, I saw warmth and kindness.

"Thank you for helping me." The words burned on the way out. I coughed a few times and felt wetness in my chest. My lungs ached with each deep breath.

"You're welcome, honey. You know, you look a lot like my baby brother," she said wistfully as she checked my IV. "He overdosed a few years ago. That's why I do this job. No one should have to lose someone they love to drugs."

She turned away for a moment and spoke to someone I didn't see. "Can you let his father know he can come in now?"

Too tired to be relieved that my father had stuck around, I closed my eyes and waited. A few minutes later, I heard the nurse telling him to sit in the chair by the bed, and I glanced at him as he put his bag on the floor. He bent over me to peer into my face.

"How are you doing, kiddo?" he asked with a smile, and I tried to smile back. I'm not sure if I quite made it, though. My brain had turned to mush at some point during the procedure. The concern in his eyes made the nausea ebb slightly because I knew that I was safe.

"M'okay, tired, groggy…," I told him and forced my eyes to stay open.

We sat in relative silence for a long time, interrupted only by the nurse who checked on me every few minutes. The nausea lessened but never completely went away, and even though I woke up completely, my body remained heavy and slow. It took about half an hour for me to wake up enough to think about Brian. I wondered what he would think if he knew the drugs were completely out of my system and that I'd be starting rehab on Monday. The request to use my father's cell phone caught at the tip of my tongue and went no further. If Brian wanted to know about my progress, he'd call.

"Dad, did you give Brian our phone number?" I pushed myself higher in the bed and felt agitated that I hadn't asked the question before.

"I didn't get a chance to, son. I'm sorry. With the rehab, and the administrators…," he started, but trailed off when he saw my face. Brian hadn't called to see how I was because he couldn't call. If my parents weren't listed, he would have no way to contact me.

"Can I use your cell phone for a minute?" I asked and held my hand out when he bent to grab it out of his bag.

"We can stop by the cellular place and add you to my plan tomorrow. You should have a phone. I never even thought about it," he said as he handed me the sleek new smartphone. It took me a few minutes to find the texting feature, but I typed in Brian's cell phone number from memory.

[Jamie] It's Jamie on my dad's phone. I'm in recovery from the detox. Just thought you might want to know it went okay.

I hit send before I could change my mind because I didn't know if he wanted to hear from me. He told me he loved me before he left the hospital. If that was true, he would want to know that I came through the procedure okay. The phone beeped almost immediately.

[Brian] I'm glad. Thank you for letting me know.

Sliding the screen up, I looked for more, but I'd read the whole message. The short, curt reply hurt more than I wanted to admit. I don't know what I expected, but I thought he'd send something more than just "yeah, thanks." With a heavy heart, I handed the phone back to my dad and rolled onto my side, facing him. Pulling my knees up, I curled in on myself. The new position actually helped my stomach, so I maintained that position and talked to my father until the doctor came in to release me.

"The doctor said clear liquids for tonight. I have some canned chicken soup we can drain, and some kind of lemon lime soda. Is there anything else that you might want? I can stop off at the market and pick up some popsicles or…," he offered, trailing off. Nothing sounded too appealing right then except a bed. I didn't know why I felt so tired after sleeping most of the day—maybe it's just that I wanted the damn day to be over. The incision on my arm itched, and I hoped that meant the implant injecting the medication into my bloodstream worked.

In our initial conversation, Dr. Lindman told me that detoxification would be the easy part. Working the program and staying clean would be harder. In my discharge instructions, he listed his phone number for me to check in on Saturday since I'd gone home and my first counseling day wouldn't be until Monday. I had no idea if I would need it. Getting high was the last thing on my mind right then, but I didn't know how I'd feel in a couple of days. For an addict looking to score, four days could be a lifetime.

I glanced at the clock on the console as we pulled into the drive and saw that it was only a little after six. The day seemed like it had lasted at least a week. Exhausted and more than a little depressed, I crawled out of the car on deadened legs. I stood off to the side while my father unlocked the back door, which reminded me that I was just a houseguest because I didn't even have a key.

"You want to watch a movie?" Dad asked, and I shook my head.

"I think I'm just going to go to bed." Brian's brush-off made my heart hurt, and I didn't feel much like company. A headache loomed;

the echo of pain made my temples sensitive, and I wanted to be asleep before it could take hold.

"Do you want to eat something before you go to bed?" A frown creased his face, and he dropped his bag onto one of the plush living room chairs as he passed. I hovered near the door and took off my shoes. Standing in the living room, it felt like someone else's house, and I didn't want to offend the host by dirtying the carpet.

"I just want to crash for a while. If I get hungry later, I'll come down and fix something." I strode to the stairs, cutting off the conversation as I practically ran up to the second floor to get to my room. Uncomfortable locking my bedroom door, I closed it and changed into a pair of pajamas that I found in one of the drawers. When Brian and I lived together, we slept naked in each other's arms. I missed the feeling of his skin against mine.

With a huge effort, I forced my mind away from the warm, sweet guy I missed in my bed. I crawled between the cold, unfamiliar sheets, closed my eyes, and prayed for sleep to come.

EPILOGUE

MITCH MAYFIELD leaned against the doorframe of his son's bedroom and watched his only child toss and turn in fitful sleep. For two years, he had dreamed of and prayed for that moment when Jamie would come home to him. He didn't even have the words to describe how empty he had felt driving back from the Center that horrible day he'd gone to get him, knowing that Jamie was alone and scared. To find out that Patsy had turned their son away when he needed them most made him wonder if he'd ever really known her at all.

The seizure had terrified him. Watching his beautiful child convulsing on the floor in a pool of vomit paralyzed him for only a moment before he remembered what they'd taught him at the hospital. He'd grabbed a pillow from the bed and protected Jamie's head the best he could as he watched the seizure, feeling completely helpless. But he had Jamie back, and he would do whatever it took to help his son. Jamie mumbled Brian's name in his sleep, and Mitch sighed softly. Jamie was an absolute mess, but together they would find a way to put his life back together. Mitch owed him that and so much more.

While he didn't know the details of Jamie's life for the past two years, he could guess from the outburst at the hospital. He mentioned the drug use, which of course Mitch already knew, but he couldn't accept that Jamie had been involved in pornography. Maybe it was naïve of him, but his son had always been a little shy, and he didn't think Jamie would take off his clothes in front of a camera like that. Mitch just didn't think it was in his son's nature to do that. But so much about Jamie had changed over the last two years; he didn't think he could trust any of his assumptions about his son.

Jamie rolled over in bed, still clinging to his second pillow as if he were a drowning man with a life preserver. It made Mitch's chest ache to see his son's pain. With absolute clarity, he could still see the little boy that Jamie used to be sleeping in that bed, clinging to an old, worn-out bear his grandmother had given him. That bear sat on a shelf over the dresser, covered in dust and forgotten by the adult Jamie, who reached across the bed in his sleep, searching for the boy who wasn't there.

While it had been a long day, Mitch felt confident that it was the start of something good for both himself and for Jamie. With the drugs out of his system, his son could start the life he should have started years ago, and for the first time in his entire career, he'd used the store of time he'd accumulated to take a two-week vacation. When Jamie woke the next day, they would start to sort out his future. His lawyer had already made the call to the Center that would secure Jamie's high school diploma. It was amazing what the threat of a lawsuit and media exposure could accomplish. After that, Jamie could decide if he wanted to go to college or a trade school. His seizures would make everything harder, and Mitch decided to e-mail Richard Schreiber to see about finding a top-notch neurologist.

Mitch had promised Jamie he would take care of him, and he would keep that promise.

Patsy Mayfield had given Mitch the choice between his wife and his son. He'd chosen without hesitation, doubt, or remorse. Jamie was the most important person in his life, and he said a silent prayer to whatever god was listening that he would be strong enough to save his son from himself.

Coming Soon
The conclusion of *Little Boy Lost*

Reunited with his father but missing the one man he loves more than any other, Jamie Mayfield attempts to put his life back together amid rehab, seizures, and the gutting loneliness of Brian's rejection. As he tries to cope, Jamie finds that relying on his friends isn't nearly as difficult as he'd imagined, and soon he can once again stand on his own two feet.

While recovering from his addiction, Jamie starts a new phase of his life at college, working to become the man Brian needs him to be. Only one question remains: Can Jamie earn Brian's forgiveness and win back his trust, or will their love be sacrificed at the altar of Jamie's demons?

Brian and Jamie's epic journey comes to a close in this thrilling conclusion to the *Little Boy Lost* series.

The Little Boy Lost series
by J.P. Barnaby

http://www.dreamspinnerpress.com

Erotic fiction is more than just moans, grunts, and physical pleasure. To J.P. BARNABY, erotic fiction consists not only of the mechanics of physical love, but the complex characters and relationships that lead to those all-encompassing feelings of need and longing. Sex without context is merely sex—but sex coupled with attraction, with explosive repercussions—that is good erotic fiction. J.P. authors all different kinds of erotic fiction including gay, straight, male, female, BDSM, sweet, romantic, and dark.

As a bisexual woman, J.P. is a proud member of the GLBT community both online and in her small town on the outskirts of Chicago. A member of Mensa, she is described as brilliant but troubled, sweet but introverted, and talented but deviant. She spends her days writing software and her nights writing erotica, which is, of course, far more interesting. The spare time that she carves out between her career and her novels is spent reading about the concept of love, which, like some of her characters, she has never quite figured out for herself.

Visit her web site: http://www.JPBarnaby.com; her blog: http://blog.jpbarnaby.com; at http://www.twitter.com/JPBarnaby for Twitter; and her Fan Page: http://www.facebook.com/#!/ pages/ J-P-Barnaby /36149609 3699. Contact her at JPBarnaby@me.com.

CPSIA information can be obtained at www.ICGtesting.com
Printed in the USA
LVOW121727060212

267333LV00001B/25/P